THE SORCERER OF MANDALA

Published by Yali Books, New York

Text copyright © 2016 by D Kalyanaraman
Illustrations copyright © 2016 by Raghava K K

Connect with us online —

www.yalibooks.com
Facebook: @YaliBooks
Twitter: @YaliBooks

ISBN: 978-0989061537

D KALYANARAMAN

ART BY
RAGHAVA KK

THE SORCERER OF MANDALA

YALIBOOKS

PROLOGUE

It happened not in a parallel world but in an orthogonal one, where credibility can be stretched even after it snaps, where disbelief not merely can be suspended, but drawn and quartered as well. It is the way with orthogonal worlds.

Imagine a mad cosmic artist, a maker of collages, mapping a normal world into another one. He makes changes that are subtly or radically different from the original, moving a piece here, changing a shade there.

Spaces, times, languages and cultures invariably get mixed up. If you moved to such an orthogonal world, you might long for a familiar parallel world.

Orum was a kingdom, albeit a village, in one such world.

Long, long ago or just a year back—depending on when you are reading it—a native of Orum was upset with her three daughters. She had *divers* arguments with them, a few dealing with unsuitability of young girls wearing cosmetics to school, many regarding food habits and many more about promiscuity.

"I wish," she shouted in exasperation, turning her eyes heavenwards, "no one in Orum should ever have to endure this. I wish no one has daughters anymore!"

Little did she realize that the heavenly Astu *devatas* had at that very moment woken up. The youngest among them uttered '*Tatha Astu*—so be it!' and promptly went back to sleep.

Unbeknown to her, another wish was being made simultaneously. That too in Orum. At that very moment, the king of Orum was entertaining envoys from the neighboring kingdoms of Akkam and Bakkam at his court. These kingdoms, by virtue of having bigger armies, were trying to arm-twist the king into signing treaties that were patently unfavorable to Orum. He was getting fed up with the persistence of the ambassadors. After a particularly grueling session, he got up and said as politely as he could, "Excuse me for a moment. I have to visit my sand pit."

Once in his private space, he let himself go.

"I don't want to see any more of them," he shouted. He continued ranting vile words. With spittle snaking down his chin, he ended thus, "I wish that Orum was completely isolated from its neighbors."

Of such synchronicities are the historical trajectories of worlds formed. That was the exact moment the younger Astu *devata* said, "So be it!" At once, Orum was physically isolated from the rest of the world by a powerful force field. The envoys found themselves outside the borders of Orum.

The eldest of the Astu *devatas* was horrified. He poked the youngest into wakefulness and demanded shrilly, "Now what have you done?"

"What?" asked the younger Astu sleepily.

"There is no redemption clause for the curses you sanctioned. You know that is against the Eternal Law."

"Curses, what curses? These were wishes that were granted. They should have been careful what they wished for, ha, ha."

"I wish your brain shrivels to the size of a pea."

"*Tatha As*...Oops! I almost said it."

"That is precisely the kind of unthinking impulsiveness I am referring to. You have just condemned the entire humankind of Orum to death. How will their progeny multiply if there are no female children?"

"Use an abacus, perhaps?"

6

The Elder's countenance looked like the stone images worshiped by his followers.

The Younger continued in a more serious tone.

"Every fortnight or so, I will let a portal open at the periphery of Orum. People who enter Orum then will have to leave within two days. Otherwise, they will be permanently trapped inside. Of course, no one else can get out. This will allow females of marriageable age to enter Orum, get married and settle there. If they want, they can even come in a procession."

Simplicity represents a state of the highest probability, the march towards which is an unalterable law of the universe. The gods, however, love complexity.

The Elder said, "That seems reasonable, though a little simplistic. Fine, *Tatha Astu*. One issue remains. The isolation also needs to be reversible under certain conditions. Don't make them too simple though."

"I have already thought of it." The Younger god smiled.

The thoughts of gods are louder than the shouted words of intelligent beings in most universes, if only to other gods.

The Elder nodded his head approvingly. "I see. Not too simple. Good...*Tatha Astu*."

Orum was changed.

CHAPTER ONE

VIKRAM

Vikram stopped at sparring distance from the master. He lowered one end of the *silambu* stick on the sand at the teacher's feet, ritually announcing that he was ready for a fight. He then bent down, took a pinch of the sand and smeared it across his forehead and chest. Ritual completed, he pushed his fears aside with conscious effort and his breathing became deep and steady. Now focused, he waited. He stared at the opponent, waited for his nod and assumed the starting position. He extended his bamboo stick upward and forward to be met by the master's. A touch stick-to-stick, and it began.

The teacher's stick slid down the length of Vikram's, imbued with a force of its own. The student countered it with a flick of his wrist. The master's stave was a blur and Vikram kept blocking the repeated forays.

"Defensive, aren't you?" shouted out the older man. "Why don't you attack?"

With a nod, Vikram went into the offensive and increased the tempo of his attack. Sweat rolled down his forehead and dripped from his unruly mop of curly hair into the thin cotton undershirt he wore. Wherever Vikram's *silambu* went, the master's followed as though the sticks were fused together.

"You seem to have found out that *silambu* is quite different from your usual sword play," remarked the master, a trifle breathless.

This gave Vikram an idea. He increased the tempo even further. His weapon now snaked towards the master's chest. As he expected, the master attempted to block the thrust and counterattack in one fluid motion.

His thrust never materialized. Vikram's feint segued into a block and continued into a lightning-fast riposte. He touched a spot on the master's bare chest with the bamboo and noted with satisfaction the surprise on his opponent's face. A bell rang out. Vikram lowered his stick and stood still, his breathing only a little quicker than before.

"That was very good," said the master, panting. "You almost hit me."

Vikram stared pointedly at the red mark on the master's chest that was getting redder.

"Well, you actually hit me," conceded the master, quite embarrassed. "Something no disciple of mine has ever managed to do."

"I just did what you taught me to do, master," responded Vikram, "I watched the technique of your fighting over many months. You invariably counterattack when I attack. So I borrowed some ideas from my sword training and decided to combine a feint, block and counter-thrust in one move."

"What you did was pretty dangerous. However, your complete lack of fear is also your greatest strength. I doubt you lack in physical strength either. Your shoulders are already broader than anyone else's in the group. I don't think I can teach you anything more. Now, it all depends on how much you practice," praised the master as he embraced Vikram. "You are turning out to be one of that rare breed of thinking fighters."

Vikram looked around to see if his brother Aditya was watching his moment of triumph. Aditya was among a small band of people standing outside the ring. The boy's eyes seemed focused on a distant point. Vikram put his bamboo away, wore the *kurta* he had taken off for the fight and walked over to his brother.

As they made their way home, Vikram put his hand around Aditya's shoulders.

"Hey, little brother. What's wrong? Did you see me bruise the master?"

"I couldn't really see very well..."

9

Vikram stopped and turned Aditya around to look into his eyes. They were red, swollen and were watering profusely.

"How long have you had this problem?" asked Vikram.

"For about a week or so. Initially, my vision was blurry at times, especially when I worked on the fine decoration on pottery. Now I have long periods when I can hardly see."

"Probably nothing serious," reassured Vikram. He paused. *Bana had similar symptoms before he went blind entirely.* "I think you should talk to Appa and see the doctor."

Daivagan will know. Time to call Kalla and Bana.

As he crossed the threshold of his house, he folded his tongue, put the fore and middle fingers of his hands into his mouth and let out three piercing blasts of whistle—one long, two short.

When the chairperson of the Guild of Anonymous Abstractors asked Kalla whether his father was a thief, he wasn't affronted. He had expected the question; the guild rarely recruited members from the outside. He said, "No, he was a pleader in the king's court."

The chairman said, "Well, close but may not be good enough."

Kalla managed to persuade the committee to give him an aptitude test. Its members were shocked at the results. In a hundred years, no one had performed so well. His disguises were original and convincing, if only a little understated; his excuses on getting caught, brilliant.

Kalla was of average height, wiry, supple and extremely fast. They unanimously voted him in as an apprentice after the chairman's prized heirloom, a solid gold bracelet, went missing and Kalla denied having anything to do with it until the decision was made in his favor.

One of many interminable training sessions was under way at the guild's grounds. A stone wall of about twenty meters high stood at one corner of the field.

The wall was smooth and there were no visible handholds. As the guild elders watched, trainees in black robes attempted to climb the wall. None of them was able to go past the halfway mark.

"Kalla!" a guild elder with a sheaf of palm leaves called out.

A figure detached itself from the milling group and ran towards the wall. It went up. Not only was Kalla halfway up in no time at all, he was doing it using only his hands. Then he simply disappeared. The elder was so shocked that he shouted out, "Kalla, where are you?"

"Here," a voice next to him answered.

"But I saw you or rather didn't see you...I mean...you disappeared."

"I simply reversed my robe halfway up the wall." He lifted up the corner of the robe.

"As you can see, I've lined the inside with cloth the exact color of granite. The pattern on it is meant to deceive the eye."

Then the signal sounded—a long whistle followed by two short notes. *That must be Vikram.*

"I'll be seeing you," Kalla shouted out as he raced away.

"This is a boy to watch out for," said the elder to no one in particular.

"Bana, take care of your little brother! I am going out and will be back in an hour. If he starts crying, put him in the cloth hammock and rock him to sleep. I have tied a rope to his waist-string. Hold on to the other end. Otherwise you won't know if he crawls away quietly."

"Don't worry," said Bana, "I'll guard him with my life."

Bana made sure that his mother left before he focused his attention on the baby.

"At least I have you," said Bana, flicking the rope in what he thought was the general direction of the baby.

"An audience of one is better than none. I hope you don't mind listening to bits of my play."

The baby gurgled.

"I have got to this important part in the play where the heroine has found the king's insignia ring. That's the one the king gave her as a token of his love—"

The baby burped. "Yes, you are right. As you say, he'd given her a baby as well as a token."

"Anyway, this ring was swallowed by a fish that was caught by an admirer who brought it to her as a—"

The baby burped louder.

"—Right, you know the story. Now this is the scene where she flourishes the ring. Should she say something profound? Or should she just throw the ring at him? More dramatic, don't you think?"

Bana felt a warm trickle at his feet. "You are one demanding critic, aren't you?" complained Bana as he went out to wash his feet.

Then he heard the signal. Two long blasts followed by a short one. *Vikram*.

Bana fumbled around a bit but managed to find the post that supported the lean-to roof. He tied the baby's waist-string to the post and was off.

Vikram waited under the thinking tree, their usual meeting point. He grabbed at a twig, broke it and threw it down in frustration.

"Hey, hey, why the violence?"

Vikram froze for a moment on hearing a voice from behind him but he recovered quickly.

"You took your time about it, didn't you?" he said as he turned around to face Kalla dressed in tight-fitting black pants and tunic.

Kalla grinned and pretended to punch Vikram. Vikram's left hand blocked the blow and his right snaked towards Kalla's face.

"Ow, that hurt. You idiot, Vik. You hit me," cried out Kalla.

"Sorry, Kalla, it was automatic. I actually pulled the punch, you know."

"Great to know," said Kalla, feeling his jaw gingerly. "If you weren't so tall, with the reach of a gorilla, I can take you down anytime."

"Oh, yeah..." Vikram rued the inadequacy of his response. However, he was saved from further repartee by the appearance of Bana.

Bana's large frame was shaking. Perspiration damped large portions of the white cotton tunic that stuck to his body at several places.

Bana puffed audibly. "I ran all the way—where is the fire?"

"Yes, why did you call us?" echoed Kalla.

"We need to do something right now," averred Vikram.

"Yes, I have an idea. Let's do some play acting. I can be the king. You can be courtiers."

"Shut up, Bana!" cut in Kalla, in the tone of one who has said it before and often.

"I know you would rather play house with Madavi." Kalla reddened.

"First it was Bana," continued Vikram as if no interruption had occurred, "now it is my brother Aditya. We have to put an end to it."

"Are you saying Aditya is also getting fat and ugly or...?"

"He is also becoming blind, like me." Bana voiced the unspoken words.

A silence followed.

"I know there has been some form of epidemic in town. We can't do anything about it," said Kalla, breaking the silence.

"There must be a reason," said Vikram, rubbing the silky down on his chin.

"I know," Bana's squeaky voice was a scale higher, "we could consult an astrologer."

"Yes, let's meet Daivagan," said Vikram. "There are other things I want to ask him first."

Vikram had already taken off before the other two could respond.

As they ran, Vikram had a nagging feeling that their lives were about to change.

Vikram bade Kalla and Bana wait at the entrance of the astrologer's house.

Daivagan's house was on a street among those of speculative futurists—betel-leaf readers, tea-leaf readers, face readers, slow readers, canine entrailologists and necromancers. His house was the most prominent of the lot with a large facade. Through the front door, you could see the other end a hundred meters away, right into the Street of Sundry Wastrels, a street that housed playwrights, authors, poets and critics of various descriptions. The door was decorated with a string of mango leaves made of beaten copper sheets and three horizontal white stripes with a red dot in the middle. On it was embedded a large brass knocker. This was, however, rarely used as the door was kept open during business hours, and Daivagan invariably shouted 'Come in' before any one could knock. Rumor had it that his great reputation for accurate prognostication grew partly because he wrote predictions *post facto* into the Gnomon. Daivagan was the keeper of the Gnomon, a book in which current happenings and future predictions were faithfully recorded.

Vikram crossed a long corridor and paused at the threshold of the main hall.

Daivagan sat cross-legged on a raised wooden seat draped in the black fur of an unidentifiable animal, in front of a large five-wick brass lamp. The oil had burnt low and one of the wicks was sputtering. A box of cowry shells lay open in front of him. Thick incense smoke curled out of a brass burner. The smell of flowers heaped on an egg-shaped icon in a niched altar added to the bouquet. A cage doubling as a wind chime hung from the dark rafters in the ceiling. Vikram felt no draft in the room; he could not be sure if the notes that sounded often enough to linger in the air came from the cage or from the song bird in it.

"Come in Vikram, I knew you would." Daivagan's voice resonated a bit before damping out.

Vikram prostrated before the astrologer in the approved way, with eight parts of his body touching the ground. He then recited his lineage-song, which traced both his bloodline and teacher-disciple roots.

"Of the disciple lineage of Arishtalali and Plutavadi
Adherent of the western branch of the mlechcha Gnomon,
Son of Kuyavan, the son of Viswakarma,
the son of Kuyavan, the son of Viswakarama,
the son of Kuyavan, the son of Viswakarama
I, Vikram, bow to you."

Vikram made the ritual obeisance to the sages of the song as he recited it. "Let me guess," said Daivagan. "Your family has a tradition of naming sons after their paternal grandfathers, right?"

"Yes, how did you know?"

Daivagan dismissed this with a shrug of his shoulders and a smile that showed tobacco-stained teeth.

"Your lineage is what you came to see me about, right?"

"Well, yes, if you say so. Actually I came to find a solution for the blindness of my brother Aditya and others, and for the isolation of Orum, *apeechiko*," replied Vikram, using the term of high reverence.

"The time has come to tell you of many things that you do not know. You are right in your suspicions. Kuyavan is not your father."

It took a while for Vikram, who hadn't suspected anything of the sort, to recover from his shock.

Daivagan paused. He dipped his right hand into a small ornate metal container and brought out a pinch of dark brown powder, which he proceeded to inhale sonorously.

"But that's not what I wanted to ask you—"

"That's enough of your impudence, young man. Young men these days have no respect for elders. What you get is what I choose to give. What was I saying, boy?"

"You were talking, *apeech*, about the circumstances of my birth," said Vikram, using the shortened form of respect. He was surprised that his voice was steady.

"This is perhaps not the place nor is it the right time to be talking about it." Daivagan grabbed a fistful of cowry shells and threw them on a mandala drawn on the ground in front of him.

"Actually, no, or rather yes, this is almost the right time to talk about it. My cowries never fail me. Okay, move a little to your left. Wait for two seconds. Good...this is now the right space-time to talk about your trip." "Why are your friends waiting outside? Call them in," said Daivagan, adjusting one of the shells and peering suspiciously.

"Don't just stand there, come in both of you!" Daivagan called out without looking up. "Wipe your feet and skip the lineage song!" he added.

Kalla and Bana joined Vikram.

"I cannot tell you the entire story. There are things that you will have to find out for yourself. You will have to take a trip out of Orum—"

"But how is that possible, *apee*, since no one born here can leave Orum? I have learned from portions of Gnomon I was permitted to read that there is a world outside the force field surrounding Orum."

Daivagan's eyes swiveled. They moved up and almost disappeared into his forehead. For a moment, only the whites of his eyes could be seen. Then his eyelids closed. His body became rigid. A light patina of sweat appeared on his forehead. When he spoke, his voice sounded deeper.

"Don't you know that everything that is destined to happen will happen? Anyway, take it from me. You will take your birthright—that is the wooden box your mother Durga has been guarding so zealously— and travel out of Orum. Beware of the forbidden forest. You will meet monsters. Some of them may eat you. There is a girl involved. Or rather many. A wild girl, an evil magicker, and many interesting and exceedingly frightening things. Ah, yes, you will find your teacher. Rather, teachers. Some may fly and some may only hover. You may save Orum from its isolation. So it may be destined."

Daivagan leaned forward and grabbed at Vikram's hands, holding them palm up, the lamp lighting the lines on Vikram's hand. "See, the mark of the conch and the wheel. You, indeed, are the chosen one."

A five-horned cicada shrilled.

"See or rather, hear the portent. What I am saying is absolutely true."

"Will I find me?"

"Aren't you here already? Don't ask stupid questions."

"Can you give us some details, *apee*?"

Daivagan stared unseeingly into the flame of the lamp. "It is very simple. Go to the gate of the enchanted entrance. Your palms will open the portal."

"I know the gate," whispered Kalla. "One of our training gigs at the guild was held there."

"Where do we go from there?" asked Vikram of Kalla.

"Do you know exactly where the place is?" asked Daivagan.

"Yes, *apeechiko*."

"What a pity! Then you will never be able to know where you are going next. It's the law. It's the Hansa-Bhargava principle of insecurity. You can never know both where you are and where you are going next. In fact, if you know where you are, where you are going is simply not defined. Anyway, that need not concern you. I am sure you will find pointers as you go along. With luck, you will succeed in liberating Orum from its curse of isolation and perhaps ensure that no more children are born blind. You may even reverse the blindness in many cases or just—"

"*Apeechiko*," Bana cried out, "do you mean to say that my blindness and the isolation of Orum are connected?"

"Yes and as I was about to say, just—"

"Then we should go," said Vikram. There was a steely determination in his voice. The five-horned cicada shrilled again.

"That's not right," whispered Bana, "Say, 'I swear by all that is holy that I shall cure this blindness', twist your head around and let the spectators see the emotions playing on your face. It will help if you seal the pact with blood by cutting your hands."

Bana jumped up as 'shuddap' sounded very close to his ears.

"Kalla, I told you not to..."

"Hey, I was just practicing throwing my voice," said Kalla, who now sounded distant.

"There are a whole lot of things about you that need to be thrown away," muttered Bana.

"As I was saying earlier," Daivagan cautioned, "just make sure that the monsters on the way do not discomfit you or worse, eat you. I am not going to mention various ordeals that await you. In any case, it does not matter because you may not survive until then. Take your box and of course, the girl..."

Vikram waited a while for Daivagan to finish his sentence. After a respectful interval, he asked tentatively,

"The girl, *apeechiko?*"

"What girl? Now you are imagining things. Off with you. I suppose you know my standard disclaimer. Normally, I take it as read. Anyway, just read it aloud."

Vikram took the palm leaf that Daivagan offered and started reading. He traced the words with his finger, lips moving and expression tormented. He read slowly.

"Anything that is predicted to happen will happen. However, there is some doubt if it will happen in this universe. It is also not true, as my son when he gets into his teens will say, nothing happens around here any more. In fact, things don't happen until you notice them, unless you notice that nothing is happening. Things predicted haven't happened only because they haven't happened yet or they haven't happened *here*. It is impossible to predict both the time and place of occurrence of an event. The better you are able to predict the timing of an event, the more unpredictable will be the place of occurrence of the event. So much so, it may take place in a universe of a different dimension."

Vikram paused for a while. "The rest of it is in very fine print. How do I read it?"

"Read it in a low voice."

He read, "Not...with...standing anything contained herein, no liability shall be incurred by the..."

"Prognosticator."

"...for any actions of the..."

"Prognosticatee."

"For any events in his/her/its life arising or otherwise from anything said or left unsaid during a reading or in passing."

Vikram let out a big sigh of relief.

"Good, you may go now. By the way, please do not shorten respect-forms more than usual," said Daivagan.

"All right, *app*."

"Come, we have work to do." They trooped out before Daivagan could respond.

"What did Daivagan mean when he said Kuyavan is not my father," Vikram wondered aloud.

"I see it," said Bana. "Something similar happens in the play I am composing. A king abandons his child and—"

"Don't be silly, Bana," cut in Vikram. "I don't think I should read too much into it. He probably meant that my father and I are very different people. I am excited that there is a possibility of ridding our village of the blindness-causing disease. And of course, if I am able to rid Orum of its isolation, there would be no more processions of unmarried girls, coming in gangs with their mothers to get engaged."

He gazed at his hand. The yellow lion tattoo seemed to mock him. He thought of his disastrous engagement with Ponni.

Earlier, he had visions of a perfect *swayamvaram*, a ceremony in which the bride chooses a groom. He pictured a demure girl, dimpling with pleasure, signaling her choice with downcast eyes before tenderly placing a garland around his neck. What happened at the actual engagement ceremony didn't quite follow this script.

Sure, the girl was stunningly beautiful, with large eyes, a lovely dusky complexion and long braided hair that she had to move out of the way before sitting down. She looked around, walked up to him and looked him over. He blushed and said, "My-my-self, Vikram. Your good name is Ponni, I suppose."

"Not much of a field. You will do, I guess." Ponni stuffed the garland into his arms and walked away.

Worse was to come. His mother Durga fawned all over her. "So sweet," she said. She actually said 'cho' and 'chweet'. Vikram couldn't bear to verbalize the words even in his mind.

He remembered his mother's parting words. "I love a child with spirit. She is so much like me. I hope marrying her will help you mend your wild ways. You are so much like your father..."

Tradition dictated that he had no choice in the matter of his engagement. The thought that Ponni was in a procession on its way to Orum made him distinctly queasy.

"So, what do you say, Vik?" asked Kalla.

"Huh?" Vikram took his gaze off the lion on his hand.

"I can see your mind is elsewhere." Kalla scrutinized Vikram's face carefully. "I see. As we speak, Ponni should be on her way to Orum."

"No, no," protested Vikram.

Kalla looked at him and shook his head. He continued, "I think it's a good idea to go on this quest that Daivagan spoke of. I too would like to be away for a while. There is this issue of a missing guild secretary's ring. It will be great if Bana can see again...though once he sees himself he may wish otherwise..."

"Kalla, we have things to do. You have to steal a few horses and weapons from the blacksmith. We leave tomorrow."

"Oh wow," Bana exclaimed, "we are going on a quest."

"I am sorry, Bana," Vikram said, placing a hand on his shoulder. "I don't think you will be able to endure the journey. When we are gone, if people ask you about our whereabouts, just say you don't know."

Bana stood with his massive arms folded across his chest as Vikram spoke to him. His mouth was a grim line.

"I am going with you. Merely because I am blind, do you think I am incapable as well? I am capable of looking after myself and others." He stopped short in some confusion as he realized that he had left his little brother alone, tied to a post.

"Come on, Bana, reconsider your decision."

"No way, Vikram. I am much more personally affected by this than the two of you. Also, it has always been my dream to be a scribe on a heroic journey."

"All right, all right," agreed Vikram. He knew Bana was generally easygoing and flexible but on this issue, he was going to be stubborn.

"We leave at dawn," said Vikram.

CHAPTER TWO

THE CASKET

Sunlight dappled through tree leaves. A light breeze streamed through Vikram's hair. Sweat trickled down his neck on to his broad shoulders.

Kalla rode immediately behind him. He sat easily on his mount, his short yet sinewy frame almost blending in with that of the horse and the skyline. Bana brought up the rear.

"Why the big hurry to start immediately?" asked Kalla. "A day or two is not going to matter."

"Well, true...I just didn't like the idea of meeting Ponni," replied Vikram, looking slightly embarrassed.

"Hot day, isn't it? I think we should rest a bit."

"Come on Kalla, we just stopped a couple of hours ago. In another hour, we should be at the portal."

"Are you saying I am tired?" scoffed Kalla. "Back at the guild academy, we were trained to ride saddleless on horses whose backs were coated with coal tar for hours on end. We were required to wear white breeches. At the end of the ride, our behinds had better be spotless. Otherwise, they got tanned. Our teachers ensured that. So this ride is no problem at all."

"Then who said we should rest a bit?" Vikram looked around and stared briefly at the large form of Bana draped over his horse. It then occurred to him that the voice sounded much closer than that.

"Hey, why should you guys be tired?" the voice continued, "After all, I am the one who is carrying you."

Vikram looked askance at his horse. "Oh my God! Kalla, you have stolen a *speaking horse!*"

"Come on. One speaking horse out of three isn't so bad and I can assure you that the swords I stole from the blacksmith won't talk." Kalla sounded upset at this affront to his professional competence.

"What about the blacksmith you locked up in a room?" Vikram looked accusingly at Kalla.

It took him a while to realize that Kalla wasn't going to answer the question. He sighed and turned to the horse. Though it seemed unnatural, Vikram steeled himself and addressed the horse.

"Fine, so you talk. What do we call you?"

"I don't have a name. I fancy the name Chetak. *That's* a horse on which you can go on adventures and rescue princesses—slim ones in distress, that is..."

"I too like the name Chetak. Surely, you mean slim *and* beautiful princesses?"

"If I have to carry two people, I don't care if they are beautiful. They'd better not weigh much."

"Now that you are carrying only one, do you really want to stop? You know we did stop at the last village."

"As far as stopping at the last village goes, I think I am going to have recurrent nighmares. Excuse the pun. When you explained that I needed new shoes, the blacksmith brought his crossbow. You should have enunciated more distinctly. If you'd said properly, 'I want him shod', he would have understood."

"Vikram, I wish you hadn't stopped him," said Kalla.

"Let's rest somewhere," said Chetak, "perhaps at that green meadow with flowers and butterflies."

"A nature lover, isn't he?" said Kalla.

"I love butterflies."

"Oh, I thought horses couldn't see in color," said Bana.

"Actually, I love their slightly acid, crunchy taste." They stopped to rest in the shade of a *neem* tree.

"Will you take this ugly satchel off my back? It seems to weigh a ton," groaned Chetak.

"Hey, those are the tools of my trade," said Kalla as he hoisted the heavy bag effortlessly off Chetak's back. Kalla's elfin face belied his immense strength.

"What have you got in there? I hope you don't have an *udumbu*. I am allergic to them," said the horse.

"What's an *udumbu*?" asked Bana.

"It's a monitor lizard used in our trade to scale high walls. You tie one end of a rope to the *udumbu* and throw it on to the top of the wall. The animal clings to it tightly. Its grip is strong enough to support a man climbing the wall. Of course, I don't need one. I can climb any wall, even ones with no visible handholds. Besides, I don't like the idea of cruelty to animals. In fact, I have proposed a clause in our guild rules to ban the use of *udumbus*."

"Let's eat, sitting around in a circle," continued Kalla.

"Since there are three of us," said Vikram, "we have no choice but to..."

"Then," said Bana, "let's sit in a triangle."

Vikram rolled his eyes. He sat down and the others followed suit.

"I have been thinking about the casket you brought along. Didn't Daivagan say it is crucial to our quest? Why don't you open it to see what is inside?" said Bana.

Vikram hesitated. It had been an impulsive decision on his part to bring the box his mother kept under her bed. She had always said, "I'll give it to you when the time comes." After Daivagan had instructed him to take the box, Vikram was certain that it was going to help them in their quest.

Bana ran his fingers over it. "This box does not seem to have a lid." He sounded squeakier than usual.

Kalla was visibly excited. To Vikram, this seemed like a prelude to an argument that Bana and Kalla were wont to have. He wasn't wrong.

"Can you call it a box if it does not have a lid?"

"You certainly can. Anything that contains something can be called a box," came Bana's quick reply.

Kalla had him in a corner now. "How do you know it contains something when you can't see what's inside it?"

"Ha, the old argument. When a tree falls in a forest and there is no one to hear it fall, does it make a sound? You can always postulate an observer and—"

"Will you two stop it?" Vikram took the casket from Bana.

The bottom was clearly marked by four small protuberances on which the box could rest. The top was inlaid in ivory with a stylized conch and a wheel. Something scratched at the doors of his memory and he bid it enter.

The conch and the wheel—Daivagan had spoken about the markings on his arm.

Instinctively, he placed the inner forearm of his right hand on top of the box so that his tattoo matched the markings on the box. Warmth radiated from his palms to his shoulders, down the sides of his back and up his spine. It turned into a flame and burned deep between his eyebrows before it splintered into myriad sparks in his head. He heard a strange buzzing as if of a dozen bees. He lost consciousness.

When he came to, Bana was bending over him. Kalla was hauling a large dripping waterskin towards him. Vikram sat up quickly before Kalla could dump the water on him.

"I guess I blacked out. Must have been the sun."

Even as he said it, he knew with certainty that something significant had occurred. The box lay open by his side. A blue silk scroll on wooden rods rested diagonally inside. Kalla pounced on it and unrolled it. The scroll was entirely blank.

Kalla's eyes lit up. "Wow, secret writings," he said, "I know how to make them visible."

In a flash, he dipped his hands into the waterskin and sprinkled some water on the scroll. Something seemed to appear on the silk cloth. Vikram took the scroll from Kalla. On close examination, he saw that it was merely the water soaking through and making visible splotches.

"I wish I'd some oil of igneous rocks and some muriatic acid..." muttered Kalla. He brightened suddenly. "Yes, application of fire. That's the er...authenticated means of entry."

"Shut up," said Vikram and held up a hand. To his surprise, his hand blurred a little as a violet beam shot out and struck the fabric. Shiny gold letters appeared on the surface.

Vikram read—

Son, you have now awakened the power of magic within. Trust in it and you will accomplish what you seek. Do not worry that you do not know precisely what you seek. In fact, it is sometimes better that way. If you know what you seek, what is the point in seeking it? Be that as it may, my blessings for your success.

PS: Don't get rid of the box as yet.

It was unsigned. In smaller letters it bore the legend—*This document does not need a signature as it is produced by magical means.*

"Let's press on," said Vikram. His mind was seething with questions.

"Vik, what's wrong with you? How can we move on now? It's so dark I can hardly see the gold filigree on your shirt. What do you say, Bana?" asked Kalla, turning to Bana.

"Darkness doesn't make any difference to me," said Bana.

"Sorry Bana, I didn't mean to ask you if you could see the—"

"Shut up Kalla, don't apologize. I am tired."

Kalla nodded in agreement and looked expectantly at Vikram.

"It's just that I don't feel like resting," said Vikram, "till Aditya is cured and of course, Bana and others, and our village is rid of the curse of isolation. I am not sure if I can sleep."

"Don't be silly, it's far too dark," said Chetak, as he lay down on his side.

"I thought horses sleep standing up," Bana's eyebrows rose in an exaggerated gesture of incredulity.

"You probably thought horses couldn't talk either," said Chetak. "Will you please let a horse sleep?"

Bana glared at what he thought was Chetak's back.

"Fine, then we rest here and ride early," Vikram pronounced.

He slept fitfully; the buzzing in his ears continued only to be interrupted by thoughts of Ponni.

CHAPTER THREE
BRAMARA

They were at the periphery of Orum just as the horizon brightened. They made their way around a large pile of rocks, perched so precariously that they seemed to defy gravity. Beyond these rocks, in the middle of nowhere, appeared gleaming bronze gates with no walls on either side.

They dismounted.

Vikram bent down, picked up a handful of pebbles and threw one of them at the edge of the gates. The pebble stopped in midair and fell down. He threw another, much harder this time. This one rebounded lightly as though from a padded wall and fell to the ground. There seemed to be no way around the force field that stretched invisibly from both sides of the gates.

The bronze gates were studded with figurines, knobs, levers and niches. Prominent among these patterns was a figure of a bull with wide curving horns, a pronounced hump and a large dewlap. There was some kind of a strange writing around the figure.

"I'm sure I've seen seals like this somewhere before," said Kalla.

"Don't be silly," said Vikram. "This is obviously a bull."

All of a sudden, Bana let out a shout. It was clear from the look on his face that he had been thinking deeply.

"Tell me," he said, his voice aquiver with excitement, "didn't we pass a large outcrop on the way? Is it casting a shadow on the ground?"

"Of course," answered Kalla without looking to check.

"I know exactly where the shadow is. I have trained to walk entirely in shadows."

"Look at the shadow of the rock on the gate!" said Bana, finding it hard to contain his excitement. "That will tell us how to open it. We just have to wait until noon and the shadow of the rock will tell us where the opening is."

Kalla went closer to inspect the shadow.

"What do you mean, Bana? There will be no shadow cast at noon." Vikram said.

"I didn't say it would be easy," said Bana with an exaggerated shrug of his shoulders.

"Ignore Bana, he has been listening to too many adventure stories." The voice sounded very near Vikram's ear. It had a faint musical twang.

Vikram twisted his neck around. There was no one near him.

"Don't worry about who I am. All you need to know is that I am here to help you." The voice spoke in his ear again.

Vikram looked suspiciously at Chetak, who raised his eyebrows, twitched his rhomboids and continued to dip into the nosebag. As Vikram looked around in bewilderment, he noticed an insect hovering near his ear.

"Oh my god, it's a wasp," he exclaimed.

"Please, not that W-word. I am a bee. A very special bee with six tongues. That way, when I suck nectar, I don't get pollen on any of my other body parts. I can be what I choose to be. Within limits, of course. I had to decide whether to be a bee or to not be a bee, but that's another story. Now, listen, take the bull by the horns."

Vikram thought he had ceased to be amazed at the kind of things that were happening around him. He shook his head to clear his thoughts. With great difficulty, he schooled his features to display nonchalance.

"Oh, you are a motivational speaker. Next you will be telling me about the time you had an incurable disease and how your faith saved you. I just need to open the gates."

"Thank God, for a moment I thought you were going to say, 'buzz off' or worse, 'you suck'."

"This is what you need to do to open the gates—take the bull by the horns."

"Oh, ah...I see."

Vikram touched the bas-relief image of the bull on the gate. To his surprise, his hands went right through and he found himself grasping the horns of the bull.

"Now twist," said the voice in his ear.

Vikram twisted.

"Say, 'open sesame'."

"Is that really necessary?"

"No, not really. But, when you do something, do it with style. It is the mantra for opening magical doorways in most universes."

"Open Sesame."

The doorway gradually became tenuous until it dissolved completely. Only a faint outline of the door frame was visible.

"Thanks, er...bee."

"My name is Bramara. You need to get a move on. The gates will remain open only for a thousand heartbeats."

Vikram and his companions entered the portal, stepped out and looked around in wonder.

CHAPTER FOUR

THE FORBIDDEN FOREST

The forbidden forest lay in front. It was thick with trees and the noise of five-horned cicadas. While the forest was dark, sunlight illuminated the landscape between the gates and the line of trees ahead.

A breeze picked up and the smell of rotting corpses assailed Vikram. It was the kind of persistent smell that hangs around at a party and asks for more wine long after most guests have gone home.

"I don't like the smell in here," Chetak's nostrils wrinkled.

"Neither do I but it gives me an idea," said Kalla. "If I can get some of this smell into my clothes, I bet pursuers on horseback will be put off."

"Why would people pursue you?" asked Bana.

"It's an occupational hazard."

"Do we have to go through this path?" asked Chetak.

"No," said Kalla, "you can go back to the portal and beat at the door with your hooves all day long, asking to be let in."

"Look at this sign!" shouted Vikram.

It was a crude map inscribed on a stone slab. 'HERE BE YALIS', it said. A single thick arrow pointed to the legend—'YOU ARE HERE'. The writing was all scrunched up to the right, indicating that the writer had miscalculated the space needed.

"From the way the writing is crowded to the right, I deduce that it is written in a left-to-right script," said Kalla, looking closely at the writing.

"What do you mean, you just read it out!" Bana protested.

"Let's just follow the path," declared Vikram, urging Chetak along.

"The inscription says something about *yalis*. What are *yalis*? Are they interesting?" mused Kalla.

"*Yalis*," said Vikram, "are probably a boring family that lived here long ago."

"I know what they are," said Bana.

"A *yali* is a monster with the beak and wings of an eagle and the body and claws of a lion. It has a long stiff tail that ends in a fang capable of injecting a large amount of venom into a victim. What they don't lack in size, they make up for in cunning. They hunt in packs. A keening of *yalis* can polish off a large herd of elephants in a heartbeat. Their age-old enemies are the *nagas*—the serpents. The reason *nagas* and *yalis* don't get along—"

Vikram interrupted Bana's talk. "That's fascinating, but save it for another day." He hadn't paid attention to what Bana had said, but had recognized the peculiar look on Bana's face and correctly surmised that he intended to go on a bit longer.

An uncomfortable silence followed Vikram's words. They moved on warily. Vikram's thoughts turned inexplicably to Ponni. *By now, Ponni should be on her way to Orum along with the procession.*

CHAPTER FIVE

THE PROCESSION

When a large number of people walk in a line, the distance between the first person in the line and the last keeps increasing, unless there is someone beating a drum or severe punishment is handed to people who break step. It is worse if the group consists of girls decked in their bridal finery, with anxious mothers chaperoning them and the leader is equipped with only a flag and a whistle.

Ponni found herself at the tail end of the procession.

A thin haze of mist lay over the forest trail leading to Orum. Pine mixed with cedar perfumed the air. It was just before dawn; overhead, stars lay sprinkled along the Great-Sword-in-the-Sky in a wide swath from west to east. The ground beneath was soft and springy with lush clumps of ingrowing Akkambian grass. Trees jutted into the trail; lichen grew in patches along the sides of the force field that isolated Orum and now enveloped those in the procession. Dayingales sang. Cricket-catchers appealed. Babblers howled and owls blabbered. Chinese-whisperers took it up, building subtle riffs until all of a sudden something completely new emerged. The euphony of song and counter-song rose, ebbed and eddied.

Ponni saw her mother Jabala at a distance, heading the line that meandered through the forest trail. Jabala held up a red pennant that fluttered in the air. She blew hard into a whistle at intervals. A long trill followed by a short one pierced the air. It was a signal for all to gather around Jabala, who had now stopped. As they moved toward her, *kanjeevaram* saris rustled, anklets tinkled and pearl necklaces swayed on young necks. Ponni stopped, allowing others to move ahead.

The line got shorter, coalescing at a distance into a small knot around Jabala. There was reason for Ponni to lag behind.

"I am not a slave," her mind shrieked at her.

"Then why are you following this group like a mindless slave?" she shrieked back. She even managed to shriek the sibilants.

She tossed her head in an unconscious gesture of rebellion. Her hair, despite being woven into a braid, was too thick and too long to follow the movement of her head.

Madavi, who had stopped to remove a thorn from her foot, turned back and started walking with Ponni. Madavi loomed a little over Ponni—she was half a head taller.

"Ponni, what's wrong?"

"I want out. I don't want to get married to an oaf."

"You should have said so at the engagement. You think all men are stupid oaves."

"Oafs?"

"Whatever. Come on, you opted to be a part of this procession. You chose Vikram at the *swayamvaram*. He appeared nice. Tall and handsome but gangly and a little too nerdy for my tastes. If Kalla hadn't been there, I might have chosen him myself."

"Kalla is a thief!" exclaimed Ponni.

"Well, he stole my heart."

Ponni groaned.

"Sorry, I couldn't resist that. But wait till I finish with him. What an opportunity! I am sure marriage will change things around for you too."

"Oh yeah? In what way? Do you think I will suddenly become right-handed? All the years of teachers rapping me on my knuckles hasn't made me change. Do you think marriage will do it? Do you also think I will instantly become fair and beautiful?"

"Come on, Ponni, don't fish for compliments. I wish I had your amazing complexion, your figure and your looks."

"Oh really? Perhaps that's why my aunt made me pack two boxes of 'White and Lovely'."

"What's that?"

"It's an ointment that you apply on your face to make it whiter. I think it contains a lot of quicklime. I will use it—over my dead body."

"You won't need to. You will be naturally pale then. Anyway, as a bride-to-be, you should be brimming over with happiness."

"If I brimmed over any further, I will be classified as an active volcano. Didn't I tell you? I don't want to get married."

"Then why did you garland Vikram at the *swayamvaram?*"

"He was the only one who didn't have a sly come-hither look. In fact, his eyes were distant. I thought he must be an introspective and sensitive person."

"I don't have your way with words. Between then and now, what has changed?"

"Nothing."

Ponni held up her hand to reveal a tattoo—a rampant lion in a field of indigo grass and a haloed sword set in stone. "Even if I am permanently marked now, I would like to exercise my inalienable right to change my mind."

"Hey, yours is a lion. Mine and Kalla's are unicorns." Madavi held up her hand as well.

Ponni pushed Madavi's hand away with some violence.

"You can have Kalla. And Vikram too. Given your abilities, maybe you can hypnotize both of them into behaving. Anyway, I am not coming to Orum. I am going back—"

Three quick blasts of a whistle interrupted her.

"This means we really have to hurry. You know your mother. Come quickly before she gets annoyed." Madavi gathered the folds of her sari, tucked the loose end at her waist and ran towards Jabala.

Madavi ran ahead, while Ponni stood rooted to the spot. Something caught her attention and made her look hard at the group again.

Initially, she missed the darkening of the skyline. It soon became apparent as the forest grew silent. A black cloud hovered over the group.

Ponni watched with growing horror as tenuous forms appeared at the edge of the clearing and slithered towards them. She heard a jumble of voices. The cloud moved closer to the group, further darkening the landscape. Jabala heaved her pennant at the apparitions, perhaps trying to shoo them away. The cloud spewed forth a sudden flash of dazzling light. The women were momentarily limned in the after-glow. The specters disappeared.

Amidst the medley of noises, Ponni heard cries of 'Victory to Pisacha Pinda! Victory to Rakta Katteri!' She reached for her bow and arrow. It was too late. The cries had faded away. Her vision was growing darker. *I am too close to the edge of the path...*

CHAPTER SIX
PONNI

The warp and weft of magical force fields are generally strong and robust. However, as it is with all fabric, a magical field too can weaken or break. There is a definite possibility—even if infinitesimal—of the threads of magic being ruptured in any given slice of space. There is, of course, the effect of deterioration with passing time. As the Indifferent Book says, 'The atrophy of the universe keeps increasing'. Eons may pass where nothing happens, but suddenly one day, a temporary discontinuity in the force field might occur.

It was one such hole in the magical force field separating Orum from the rest of the world that Ponni fell through.

When neurons in your head brush past particles of magic, it takes a while to recover. When Ponni came to her senses, she wished she hadn't. She felt cold. She shivered. *Was this really happening to her?* She squeezed her eyes tight and opened them again. It didn't help. She was still in a dark and intimidating forest. There was no sign of the path on which she had come.

She heard sounds of gnawing and digging. She knew they were rodents of some kind. That in itself was not a problem.

Where there are rodents, there are bound to be snakes.

Snakes!

Ponni was ten. Even at that age, she was the star pupil in her mother's **marma** *arts class and could defend herself against fully grown men. Her mother had no problem in leaving her daughter alone when she was away visiting.*

*On one such occasion, a snake charmer had come to Akkam. He had a basket containing numerous snakes. He halted in front of her house to perform his act. Ponni watched with a mixture of fascination and dread as the charmer made the snakes sway to his music. Later that evening, as she settled into her bed, she was horrified to see a cobra at the entrance to her room. The snake raised its hood to attack her. She watched as though it were a painting—the spectacle-marking on its hood, beady eyes, forked tongue and drawn-back fangs. She screamed, jumped up and grasped an **uri,** a rope structure that hung from the ceiling in which her mother placed pots of curds and butter. She spent the whole night suspended, while the reptile looked on. When her mother returned from her trip the next morning, the snake had disappeared. Ponni was delirious and hot to the touch. She took a week to recover.*

I have to move.

She got up with some difficulty and walked unsteadily along a trail that led deep into the forest. Now and then, a patch of darkening sky came into view. Soon, it started raining. It was only a drizzle but water dripping from the trees made it worse.

On one side of the trail was an old abandoned temple. Its dilapidated columns barely supported its roof. Ponni decided to take refuge at the temple until the rain abated. The pillars had exquisite carvings on them. Some depicted elephants, some dancing women and others lions. One pillar showed lions astride elephants. Ponni could identify the fish insignia of an ancient Pandya king on one of the walls. *Kings those days built some magnificent ruins,* she thought sleepily. She went inside, shook off the rainwater from her hair and sat on the granite floor. With her eyes half-closed, she leaned against a pillar.

In a state of semi-wakefulness, she saw two birds perched on one of the broken slabs. She thought they were *kokila* birds, but couldn't be sure. One bird was completely still and seemed to observe the other's movements keenly. The other one sang, hopping and fluttering her wings. Notes cascaded—no two alike. The scene touched something deep within her.

She felt a sense of calmness...until she heard a sound of something moving. Ponni looked around for the source of the sound. What she saw terrified her.

In a semicircle around her were a dozen shiny translucent snakes. They were much larger than any she'd ever seen. A large diamond-like jewel gleamed atop each of their crowns. The jewels emitted a white diffuse light that made them visible even in the dark.

Each one of the snakes when uncoiled was at least twenty hands long. Had Ponni been standing, the snakes' heads would have been above hers. They were a few yards away from her, just out of striking distance, hoods spread wide. Their tongues flicked in and out and they swayed from side to side, seemingly to music that only they could hear. They were getting closer.

She looked up instinctively to see if there was anything above that she could hang from to save herself. There was nothing—not even an *uri*. She told herself with determination, '*You have nothing to fear but fear itself*'. She couldn't help that snakes also entered the equation. This meant that on top of the snakes, she had to deal with fear and the fear of fear.

Ponni started to focus. The *marma* martial training from her mother kicked in. She rose up, drew the cosmic power into her abdomen and released it with a loud shout.

"HUUMM!"

Nothing happened. The snakes continued slithering forward with their hoods raised. As though on cue, all of them swayed back together—clearly poised for a lethal strike.

CHAPTER SEVEN
YALIS

They rode in a single file through the forest.

"Did you hear it?" Vikram cupped his ears and turned around to look at Kalla. Kalla's horse was trotting along riderless.

Vikram brought the horse to a halt by pushing himself deep into the saddle and gently tugging at the reins.

"Why have you stopped?"

God, another speaking horse!

Vikram decided to be nonchalant about it.

"Where is Kalla? You haven't dropped him along the way, have you?"

One moment the horse had no rider. The next, Kalla appeared on saddle, grinning.

"Why are you talking to a horse that can't speak?" enquired Kalla, grinning even wider.

"Where were you a moment earlier?" asked Vikram, ignoring Kalla's banter.

"Oh, that was a trick," beamed Kalla. He stretched himself fully. "I was merely practicing the art of becoming invisible. You want to know how it is done, don't you?"

"No," said Vikram.

"Note the color on this side of my robe. It is almost the exact color of this chestnut. I simply reverse it and flatten myself against the side of the horse. Of course, this takes a lot of practice. The guild holds a competition every year and every year without fail, I—"

Vikram had already ridden ahead out of earshot. Kalla hung back a little till Bana joined him.

"Vikram was trying to tell us that he had heard something. He didn't complete what he wanted to say. Did you hear anything, Bana?"

"I hear everything. Ever since I became blind, my hearing has become even more acute. I am sure I heard some high-pitched sounds. I have been thinking..."

Kalla guessed what was coming and tried to move away. He wasn't fast enough. Bana's hand fastened on the necklace of black beads that Kalla wore. He was forced to ride alongside Bana.

"I was just wondering what posterity will call me. Do you think 'Bana, the blind bard of Orum' sounds dramatic enough or better still 'The Brilliant Blind Bard'?"

"Bana, the buffoon of Orum, sounds just about right."

"You know what I am working on now, right?"

"I hope you are working on keeping your weight down."

"I am working on a unique play. I have thought of a brilliant storyline. There is this king who meets the love of his life at a hermitage. He marries her and gives her his signet ring as a token of his love—"

"I think Vikram needs me. I have to ride ahead." There was desperation in Kalla's voice.

The hand at his neck remained steady.

"In fact," continued Bana, "the king gave her more than that. He gave her a child."

Kalla gave up all hope of escaping from Bana and resigned himself to his fate.

"Imagine the scene as they are parting. The girl looks back, lifting up her heel, pretending that she has a thorn in her foot..." Bana droned on.

They rode for an hour or so. Approaching a clearing in the forest, they heard the sounds from before—it was high-pitched laughter. It came from all around them, gathering in volume.

Then came a rush of wings. The dreaded forms of *yalis* hurtled towards them from the sky through an opening in the forest canopy.

Bana remembered what he had read. A keening of *yalis* bearing down on intended prey is one of the most horror-inspiring sights on the planet. Worse than that is the sight of them feasting on said prey. There are few messier eaters.

Four *yalis* streaked down in a V-formation. Vikram drew his sword.

"We are all going to be eaten alive," wailed Chetak.

Bramara's constant buzzing forced Vikram to pay attention to the bee, even though his eyes were riveted on the diving *yalis*.

"This is a bit of occidental magic. Quick! Repeat after me," the bee said.

"Dei."

"Dei," repeated Vikram, in a daze.

"Ex machina."

"Ex machina."

Instinctively, Vikram extended his arms in an arc, sword pointing in the general direction of the *yalis*.

Nothing happened.

"Don't worry Vikram, it always takes a while to lower the go—"

There was a clap of thunder and a puff of smoke. The *yalis* disappeared. At the same time, Vikram's forearm tingled. The engagement tattoo glowed briefly.

A single golden feather spiraled down lazily. As it reached the ground, Vikram saw that a note was attached. He asked Kalla to read it aloud.

Thank you. When you need us, burn this. We will appear.

Bana's nose wrinkled. This always happened when he was thinking.

"I think this feather is dangerous. Let's destroy it, let's burn it," he said.

Vikram and Kalla stared at him in disbelief as they mounted their horses to continue the journey.

CHAPTER EIGHT

ORUM'S COUNCIL

The council of Orum gathered in the town square—really a circular platform with a banyan tree at the center. Kuyavan, Vikram's father, had gone around the village the previous day, beating a drum and delivering the summons for the meeting.

"The situation is completely out of control," declared Mootha, considered the eldest in the village. There were others who were older but none who were mobile and in reasonable possession of their senses.

"Something needs to be done," he continued. "In our times, hardly one in twenty children developed blindness. Now, a fifth of the youngsters between the ages of five and fifteen are blind."

Kuyavan looked grim. "The issue is personal and even more worrisome now," he said, "Aditya is developing signs of blindness. I took him to our physician. The prognosis is bad. He is likely to be totally blind in a week. My son Vikram is missing. Daivagan has assured me that he is on a mission to find a cure and would come back soon."

"I have been researching this issue for some time," said Bhautik. "I have studied data from raw Gnomonic records. It is true that the incidence of blindness is increasing at an alarming rate. It is my estimate that in ten years' time, all children will either be born blind or become blind during their lifetime."

The blacksmith nodded in agreement. "The situation is grim. Why do you think this is happening?"

Daivagan answered, "I believe it is because the men in Orum are isolated. As you know, no man has ever come into Orum from outside. If this weren't bad enough, there is something else. I suspect some extraneous factors are at work."

"What kind?" asked Mootha.

"You know that the physical body is constructed according to the plans laid down in the life codes. I believe that the force field interacts with the inherited life codes causing blindness."

"While Orum changed long ago, only now are the ill effects being felt," added Daivagan.

"But what about those who come from the outside in a marriage procession? Every time someone from Orum marries a girl from the outside, don't you think the effects are diluted?" queried Kuyavan.

Daivagan considered the question for a while. "That's a good question. Bhautik and I think that the problem is that in all cases the males belong to the village. The blindness is perhaps inherited by the son from the father."

"I agree with Daivagan," said Bhautik. "As a matter of fact, I believe that if the afflicted persons are outside the influence of this strong field, they may actually recover."

"Are you saying that the only solution is then to leave Orum, which in any case, we cannot?" asked Kuyavan.

"We need to somehow be able to remove the force field," said Bhautik, "and this needs to be done quickly. I reckon that we have only weeks or at the most a month to shut the field down. Otherwise, the conditions are likely to become permanent."

A brief lull in conversation followed. Daivagan resumed.

"No need to despair. There is hope. As we speak, young men from our village including Kuyavan's son Vikram are on a mission to seek ways by which our kingdom can be freed from this curse."

"I know," said the blacksmith. "I let them steal my horses and swords as Daivagan asked."

CHAPTER NINE

PONNI IN THE FOREST

One moment, the snakes were poised to strike Ponni; in the next, there was pandemonium. Her tattoo became unbearably hot. The snakes swung around sharply even before she heard the high-pitched keening of *yalis* and the strong beating of wings. The snakes catapulted themselves into the air. *Yalis* and snakes pursued each other between trees and on the ground. In their wriggling, fluttering and hissing, the snakes and *yalis* were indistinguishable. *This is my opportunity.* Ponni's training came to the fore and she fled the scene. The one dominant thought in her mind was to put as much distance as possible between her and the melee.

Trees flashed past like dark shadows as Ponni sped through the forest. The shrill sounds of birds ahead of her sounded shriller. *There ought to be a scientific explanation for this.* Even the sledging of cricket-catchers held a menace, a demand rather than an appeal. Crunchy, squishy sounds under her sandals sent a wave of revulsion from her toes to her head. Unbeknown to her, a rare mutation that held the hope of eternal life for all life forms in the future was squished into nonexistence, never to appear again in any universe.

There were also other kinds of unidentifiable sounds.

God, these things don't just go bump in the night, they go chadhak-chadhak and even damaaal-dumeel.

Ponni continued to run.

The forest appeared to close in behind her. The smell of rotting corpses that was pronounced when *yalis* made their appearance seemed to follow her. Despite her training, as she ran, her even breaths turned to big breaths, big breaths into gasps and gasps into choking implosions.

Just when her lungs were about to collapse, the atmosphere changed subtly. The trees turned healthier and greener. A faint smell of jasmine permeated the air. A cow grazed serenely beyond an iron gate.

As she neared the gate, things changed and the air seemed to hold a menace again. The cow, which until now was tucking into the grass, looked up and pawed the ground. Ponni thought it growled. The cow charged with its head lowered.

Dehydrated and exhausted, Ponni tried to summon her strength. It stayed hidden. She managed to strike the pose of the *hidden tiger* as she crouched down. She nocked an arrow and drew the bow. She waited for the moment she could see the whites of the animal's eyes.

CHAPTER TEN

SAGE DWIPADA

As the charging cow reached the gate, Ponni stood up and took a step back. The bovine halted her charge and blocked the entrance.

"Oh my god!" breathed Ponni.

"I am not your god though people do worship me."

Relief loosened Ponni's tongue.

"You are a cow and you talk. I am too tired to be amazed. The way you are looking at me, I should probably say 'take me to your leader'."

"MU," the cow raised its head and bellowed.

Even in her exhausted state, Ponni wondered how the cow was able to bellow out a word that didn't have a long vowel sound at the end.

"Hey Gauri, did you just call someone?" asked Ponni.

"Listen, my name is not Gauri. As you should now know, not all cows in the universe are called Gauri or Lakshmi. My name is Kamadenu. Besides, you have the advantage of me."

"What do you mean? You are the one who is in an enclosure. You also have the high ground..."

"I mean, what is your name?"

"Ponni. How is that an advantage? You mean if I know your name, I can use it to cast a magic spell over you?"

"Here comes my master, Sage Dwipada," said Kamadenu, gently shaking her head. She moved away while still staying within earshot.

Sage Dwipada was lanky and glowed a little. He sported a beard that covered most of his face and reached up to his navel.

His matted locks were tied above his head in a knot. He wore a bark cloth around his waist that was kept in place with vines. He held a spouted water pot made of brass in one hand and a short stick with a wide armrest on the other.

"Who are you, my child?"

When Dwipada spoke, words seemed to come from somewhere deep within him. Ponni assumed that this was because she couldn't see his lips move behind his thick beard. She noted with surprise that his feet didn't touch the ground. He hovered some three inches above.

Ponni folded her hands in obeisance and said, "I am Ponni, daughter of Jabala."

"And Jabala is your mother, I presume."

"Yes, and—"

"Who, may I ask, is your father?"

"I do not know. Whenever I ask my mother that question, she gives me different sets of names to choose from. I think she does not know though she thinks it might have been a good-looking flautist."

"Why would that be?" asked Kamadenu.

"Apparently, he played music for her and even the pauses were filled with melody."

"I understand," Dwipada nodded sagely, "pregnant pauses."

The expression on Dwipada's face softened.

"I like your habit of telling the truth."

"How are you sure she is telling the truth?" whispered Kamadenu in a loud aside to Dwipada.

"If your mother told you she wasn't sure which bull was your father, would you advertise it? She is obviously telling the truth. The truth is irrelevant to me. The fact that she is telling the truth is relevant," Dwipada whispered back equally loudly.

"I know it is the truth, Ponni," Dwipada continued, "because I can see the pasts, present and futures. You look exhausted. Come with me!"

"Pasts?"

"Yes, there is a multiplicity of them. For instance, I know you were a blue praying mantis in one of your earlier births."

"The current birth, however, must have been noble as you have stuck to the truth and introduced yourself as Jabala's daughter."

"I know I am tired and I am not thinking too well but it seems to me your feet aren't touching the ground. Unless..."

"I never wear high heels," said Dwipada. They are bad for your back. My feet don't touch the sinful earth because of the power of my penance."

Ponni could no longer focus on what was happening around her. However, she kept pace with sage Dwipada.

"This," said the sage with a sweep of his arm, "is my humble *ashram*."

Ponni could see greenery everywhere. A large thatched cottage was flanked by four other smaller ones. Another building, obviously a cowshed, completed the picture.

Just as she entered a cottage, she saw a pair of parrots on the porch. They were arguing like humans. She stopped, astounded.

She realized that the topic was an abstruse philosophical concept in epistemology. One of the parrots was arguing that direct perception was the best source of knowledge. The other was favoring inference as a better source. Soon the debate got too complex for Ponni to follow, especially as she was fatigued.

She thought she spotted deer wandering about. *No, I haven't. It is already spotted.*

This brought her to a moment of wakefulness. "My mother..." she mumbled just before entering her room.

"Tomorrow," averred Dwipada, "you will get answers to all your questions. Tonight, you sleep well. Do not think about your mother or Pisacha Pinda."

Pisacha Pinda? Now where did I hear this? Yes, when mother disappeared.
She was too sleepy and tired to think any further.

CHAPTER ELEVEN

PISACHA PINDA

Behind every successful man is a woman, repeatedly kicking his backside. It wasn't entirely so with Pisacha Pinda. There was one, unfortunately she never took her foot to his backside. Quite the opposite.

Sage Pinda, husband of the guilty party, not to be confused with his son Pisacha, was a happy man, or so people thought. He had his own *ashram* with some of the most prominent *asuras* as disciples. He led a simple life, subsisting on roots and vegetables. He had a wife whose duties included cleaning the *ashram* and looking after his daily needs. The only problem that preyed on the sage's mind was the lack of progeny. For a thousand years, Pinda and his wife tried desperately to have a child. They tried every other year, but to no effect.

Finally, he decided to perform a Penance of Five Fires to appease Brahma. Even after a thousand years, Brahma did not appear. The heat of the penance, however, reached the abode of Indra, the king of gods, and had him worried. He had reason to be. Someone with that kind of penance power could easily produce a virtuous son who could aspire to Indrahood.

Pinda was also worried. He almost lost his head. In a fit of desperation, he was about to sever his own head and consign it to the sacrificial fire when Brahma suddenly appeared.

What he did not know was that Indra had persuaded his queen Sasi to take the form of a small insect and sit on Pinda's tongue.

Brahma gave the sage a standard choice of boons—a thousand evil wastrels or one dutiful, intelligent son. Pinda's tongue was not under his control. He tried to say, "One dutiful, intelligent son." However, "one evil wastrel," was what he actually said.

"*Tatha Astu*—so be it," said Brahma and disappeared.

Thus was Pisacha born.

Even for a *rakshasa*, Pisacha was a violent child. Throughout his childhood, his mother kept making excuses for him. "He was abused as a child in his previous birth," she said when his school teachers or irate parents of his classmates complained.

Pisacha was personification of evil as he grew up —he pulled wings off flies, killed his parents, talked in class and later, followed the left-hand path, the path of evil. He went on to grab riches from his neighbors and undertook contracts for destroying *ashrams* and disturbing sages' penance.

Soon, he realized he needed a permanent residence to house the people he abducted and enslaved. The finest architects on the earth were commissioned to build Pisacha's castle. They conceived it as a luxurious pleasure palace of white marble. Four minarets flanked a central domed structure on a raised platform, surrounded by exquisite gardens. Pisacha's incessant interference with the architects transformed it into a different structure altogether. Marble was replaced with granite of assorted colors to provide camouflage. The beautiful onion shape of the dome was serrated and louvered to allow troops to be hidden. The elegant minarets were changed into rectangular structures with slits for crossbows and openings for dumping vats of tar and boiling oil. These structures were connected at the top with each other and the central dome. The tree-lined reflecting pool leading to the grand entrance in the original design was converted into a moat with crocodiles in it. A high wall was constructed along the inner perimeter of the moat. Seven more concentric walls were built. The most sinister feature, however, was hidden underground.

It was an altar to Rakta Katteri, a fearsome goddess who demanded human sacrifice.

Pisacha's room was adjacent to the underground temple. In the middle of this room was a raised platform, covered with a rug made of various animal skins stitched together. Pisacha boasted that the skins were culled from the last representative animals of their species on earth. In front of the platform rose a hollow pentagonal altar built of burnt bricks. A garland made of human skulls hung from a nail on a wall. A pile of skins with a cylindrical leather pillow on top formed Pisacha's bed. To one side of the room was a table with a black obsidian top and a chair made entirely of human thighbone. A gleaming spherical crystal sat on the table. An unidentifiable charred mass lay smoking in the altar; an acrid smell hung heavy in the room.

Pisacha was tall. He looked almost gaunt as he lay sprawled on the chair. The absence of a nose gave his face a ghoulish appearance. His upper lips were permanently drawn up in a sneer.

Abhishtu, Pisacha's faithful minister stood next to him, hands crossed and head bowed as Pisacha looked at the scrying crystal and gloated.

"He, he, he, he..."

"Sounds much better now, sir," said Abhishtu, looking up and desperately trying to unsquint his eyes. "Will you teach me too to gloat, sir?"

"Shut up!"

Abhishtu had touched a particularly sensitive nerve of his. More likely an entire ganglion.

Pisacha remembered how he had been rejected for a villain's part in his school play because he could not laugh.

"It should be full-throated," his master had said. "The belly should quiver and the shoulders should shake. Maybe in a couple of years' time, I can give you the part of a slave who fans the king with a fly whisk from behind the throne. For now, I am afraid you can't contribute to the play."

"Even while watching the play, I suggest you sit at least ten rows away. HA, HA, HA...HAH," the master had gloated, his shoulders shaking and the folds of his stomach quivering like jelly during an earthquake. True, Pisacha had taken his revenge later by stuffing the master head first into an earthen pot that served drinking water for the entire school, but the slight lingered.

He brought his mind back to the present with an effort.

"Let's take a look at the island," he said.

The scrying crystal rotated. The display changed. It now showed an aerial view of a pentagon-shaped island. It zoomed in on a fort on the southern side, focusing on its massive gates and walled inner courtyard.

Pisacha noted with relish that a number of women were gathered in small groups. They seemed to be talking animatedly.

"What are they saying, master?"

"Shut up and touch the left side of the globe."

Abhishtu reached out. "Ow, that is hot, boss."

"Don't worry, that's only the residual static magic that is causing global warming."

The display on the crystal changed and it now showed an image of a female form seated on a saber-toothed tiger.

"Mother," Pisacha whispered, "you will be pleased. I have much in store for you. Lots of blood. Soon you will be satiated."

CHAPTER TWELVE

AT THE ASHRAM

Ponni was still in a groggy state; she could hear the parrots arguing with each other. It took her a while to become fully awake. She found herself on a straw mattress covered with animal skins. The sun was high over the horizon. The smoke of *homa* fire perfumed the air. She found some fruits and boiled roots on a large banana leaf placed by her side. She ate quickly.

"I hope you are feeling better," spoke Dwipada from the doorway.

"Thank you very much. Now I must—"

"Go in search of your mother and the others?" The beard shook in unison with his words.

"How did you know?"

"I told you I know the pasts, present and futures, though my memory isn't what it used to be. I keep forgetting many possible bits of the future. It is, of course, better than what I will remember. Anyway, I can help you. I can tell you, for instance, that your mother and her companions have been abducted. I can tell you many more things. Do you know where you are and what dangers await you outside? Come, let us go around the *ashram* while we talk."

Ponni's face was set in grim determination.

"I suspected that she had been kidnapped. I am not going to just sit here and complain about it. She will expect me to rescue her, which is exactly what I aim to do. But first, I have a few questions to ask of you."

They walked out of the cottage together.

"Who are you? Who spirited her away? I thought I heard a name before I blacked out. I have more questions..."

"I will explain everything. Don't interrupt."

Abruptly, his mien changed. His face took on an unholy pallor. He was almost shouting now.

"If you interrupt me, you will be born as a..."

His mood changed again. "Sorry, I got carried away. I was about to put a conditional curse on you. This would have been a huge debit to my powers acquired through penance."

"Debit?"

"Sorry. Reduction. I am going to be an accountant in one of my future births."

He scratched his beard with his wooden armrest.

"Now, where was I? Yes, I have mellowed a lot and haven't cursed anyone in centuries. I also haven't had much human contact. In fact, the only company I've had is Gauri."

"Gauri? You mean Kamadenu?"

"I call her Gauri. Anyway, here at the *ashram* I have done penance for ten thousand years. The last thousand years was the Penance of Five Fires."

"Five fires?"

"Yes, I lit four fires around me. The sun burning down was the fifth. I performed the rituals and Brahma appeared before me and granted me boons."

"And you asked for immortality?"

"No, that's the one thing that gods are explicitly forbidden to grant. Long life is something else though. Apart from that, I asked for and received the Chintamani, the wish-fulfilling jewel. I could get whatever I wanted by holding the jewel in my hand and making a wish. Of course, I had to recharge the jewel every time after making a wish with the power of my penance..."

"What does all this have to do with my mother? Can you tell me where she is held?"

"DON'T INTERRUPT," shouted Dwipada but continued in a softer tone, "I am coming to that. Pisacha Pinda stole the jewel."

They walked on in silence. Ponni looked around. Two large stone blocks jutted out of the ground. One stone had a gently sloping top surface used for washing clothes. The other was rough-hewn and much smaller. Ponni almost bumped into the stones. "Why are these stones here in the middle of the pathway?"

Dwipada answered with a sigh.

"I was hoping you wouldn't ask me. This is my wife. I cursed her into a stone. And before you ask, the washing-stone is a disciple of mine...Asadu, I think that was his name. I can't remember what I cursed him for."

"No, no, I was wondering why you cursed your wife."

Dwipada hadn't seemed to have heard the question.

"After I acquired the Chintamani from Brahma, I went about making er...home improvements at the *ashram* with the help of the gemstone."

Dwipada took a deep breath before he continued. "Pisacha, who fancied the jewel for himself, plotted to steal it. He entered the *ashram* when I was away at the river taking my morning dip. He altered his appearance magically to look like me and tricked my wife Aiyo into revealing much more than where we'd hidden the Chintamani. He then stole it. After I returned from the river, Aiyo realized that something was wrong. She begged for my forgiveness. By then, Pisacha was far away and beyond the reach of my curses. However, he paid through the nose for his sin, ha, ha. The loss of his nose actually improved his face. That's when I lost my head and petrified Aiyo. I also lost at least six thousand years of penance. Of course, when she begged for forgiveness in the small interval before curses take effect, I added the clause that she would be freed from her state when Pisacha dies."

"You said the stone Chintamani needs to be recharged periodically. Does Pisacha too possess the power of meditation to recharge the stone?"

"Hah, that fraud? He couldn't meditate even if you poked him in his third eye with a thousand-petaled lotus containing a diamond. He uses alternate methods to recharge the stone."

"What he uses instead," he continued, "is the freshly-spilled blood of virgins, which is why he has kidnapped your mother and others who were with her."

"But...you said virgins."

"One of the definitions for a virgin in the Gnomon is—a virgin shall have no more than six children, not counting immaculate conceptions and no more than three lovers, at least not at the same time."

"Revered sage, where is my mother now? I need to save my mother and the other, er...virgins."

"Don't worry, Ponni. You will have help in this. As we speak, there are three young men who are on their way—"

"Hah, I don't need help from them. Anything young men can do, I can do better. Can you do something? Some long-distance cursing, perhaps?"

"No Ponni, I can't. Curses follow the inverse-square law and get very weak at long distances. Also, I don't want my powers drained. In fact, the last time I cursed was hundreds of years ago. One my disciples was disrespectful and I cursed him to become a Brahmarakshas. He is still roaming the forest, eating the occasional traveler."

CHAPTER THIRTEEN

THE BRAHMARAKSHAS

It had been waiting a long time. It was hungry, its last meal in danger of becoming a faint memory. It tried to regurgitate the memory and savor the taste. It remembered the dry, slightly acidic taste of the old Indic scholar that brought back memories of discussions on abstruse aspects of grammar. In fact, he was not particularly thin as scholars go, and he had not gone completely. Both of these created problems for Iti, the Brahmarakshas.

With most humans, Iti did not have to use up its three questions. It remembered fondly how the last person it met blurted 'I don't know anything' and it gobbled him up, no questions asked.

Half dreaming, it sat under a tree and waited.

Vikram whistled as he rode. Bana and Kalla were a length behind, and from their alternating raised voices, it was clear their debate was going nowhere.

"Why is Chetak shaking his head?" asked Bana.

"If the whistling had some semblance of a tune or wasn't so piercing, I wouldn't have to try to get it out of my head," said Chetak, without breaking stride.

For a moment, Kalla did not react. Then he looked at Bana with amazement. "You could see that?" he shouted.

"Yes," said Bana happily.

Vikram stopped abruptly.

This cannot be happening!

"You can really see? How many fingers?" asked Kalla holding up three fingers of his right hand.

"Shut up, I really can see," said Bana.

There was a sparkle in Vikram's eyes. When he spoke, his voice quivered in excitement.

"Do you realize what this means," cried Vikram. "There must have been something in Orum which prevented you from seeing. Now that you are beyond the influence of the force field you are able to see. Or maybe, there is something special about this place that enables you to see."

"You were right the first time," said Bramara, flying in to settle on Vikram's shoulder. "The magical field at Orum, where it is concentrated, can interact with your very cellular structure, preventing you from seeing. And do you know what that means?"

Vikram's face was flush with excitement.

"YES," said Vikram.

For once, Bana was speechless.

They seemed to sit straighter on the saddle as they rode on. Even Chetak's stride seemed to have an extra spring in it.

Gradually, the path narrowed. They brushed past foliage on both sides. The ambient light, which until then was sufficient for them to see their way, grew dimmer. They moved on in a single file.

At first, Vikram only saw a huge tamarind tree to one side of the trail. A little later, he could see a form under the tree.

Even while seated, the Brahmarakshas' head was level with Vikram's. The creature had wrapped its thick muscular tail around the tree trunk twice, with its end dangling from a branch.

Vikram felt a momentary flash of fear. His hand reached out to the sword at his side.

Kalla's horse suddenly appeared riderless.

"Watch out, that's a Brahmarakshas," the bee buzzed in Vikram's ears.

"Look at its tail, horns and hairy face. That's for sure a Brahmarakshas," cried out a visibly excited Bana.

"That's me. Call me Iti, while you can still talk," said the Brahmarakshas. As Iti spoke, his tail slid down from the tree trunk and fell across the path. Vikram watched with fascination as Iti's head moved up and down with its upper jaw as it spoke.

Chetak moaned softly and tried to move back.

"Stop doing that," Vikram snapped, "if you attempt to bolt, I will pin your ears back and tie a loud *mithai*-pink ribbon to it."

Chetak stopped.

"I know you are out there somewhere, Kalla. Please show yourself."

The horse that seemed riderless a moment before was no longer so. An embarrassed Kalla showed up.

Vikram turned to face the Brahmarakshas.

"I know all about you and your ilk. Ask your three questions now and let us be on our way." Vikram's voice bore no trace of fear.

"There are some formalities to be completed before that." A strange look came into Iti's eyes. It reminded Vikram of the expression on his *silambu* master's face while sparring with a beginner.

"You do know there are terms and conditions? For instance, I could ask three questions—if ever I get that far, haha—of each of you or I could put these questions to all of you. If I ask them individually, you will obviously not be allowed to consult with each other."

Bramara spoke softly in Vikram's ear. Vikram's face took on a crafty look.

"We choose that you ask the question of the entire group. Any of us can contribute to the answer. Is that agreed?" asked Vikram, sitting straighter than before on his saddle.

"That's not what I said," Bramara whispered urgently into Vikram's ear.

"I know," said Vikram.

"Deal," said Iti, spitting on its hands. "Let me start."

"Wait, there is more," said Vikram, "You must allow us to ask you a question."

Iti seemed to hesitate a bit.

"You are in no position to negotiate but I love a challenge. So be it. You may ask me only after I have finished asking two questions, that is, if you last that long. The game is over the moment you are unable to answer any of my questions."

"And if you can't answer our question, you will let us go," said Vikram.

"Deal," said Iti.

"Deal," echoed Vikram, spitting on his hand.

They smacked hands together.

Vikram wiped the gob off his hands on Chetak's mane. They waited for Iti to speak.

"This is a riddle. If you don't answer in five minutes or if you give me a wrong answer, I get to gobble all of you up, and that includes you too," said Iti, looking straight at Chetak.

Chetak cowered.

"Just skip the preliminaries and get to the riddle, will you?" said Vikram.

"Right, here goes," said Iti.

"Gada gada, gudu gudu,

Hole in the middle.

Who am I?"

The group went into a huddle.

"It is Iti, the Brahmarakshas," whispered Bana.

"Shut up Bana, we are all thinking," said Vikram.

"I know," said Kalla, "he is a guild member who talked too much and was terminated."

Bramara was barely audible when he whispered.

"This is an ancient riddle which was popular among humans many thousands of years ago. The answer is simple."

61

"How do you know the answer if it was asked thousands of years ago?" asked Bana.

"Never mind that now. It is a grinding stone. *'Gada gada gudu gudu'* refers to the noise a pestle makes when it is rotated inside a grinding stone. The answer is a grinding stone for making rice batter."

"Grinding stone for making rice batter," said Vikram aloud.

Was there disappointment writ large over Iti's face? It was hard to tell in the uncertain light.

"That was a loosener," said the grinning Iti.

"Beware the smile of a pretty woman and the grin of a Brahmarakshas. Old saying," said Bana.

"Nervous, are we? Well, well. Now for the second question," Iti paused. The grin became broader and more grotesque.

"What is it that goes in the morning on four legs, during the day on two, in the evening on three and at night on eight?"

"Do you think it is a wounded spider that gets worse and then better?" asked Bana in a low voice.

Kalla cast him a look which said it all.

Vikram looked thoughtful. "No, no. I have heard this from my mother, who had in turn heard it from a friend of hers."

"Oh yes, I remember," said Bramara.

Kalla looked at Bramara in puzzlement.

Vikram's face cleared. In a whisper, he said, "I have got it."

"Iti," he said loudly, "are you sure this is the question you want to ask? Seems a bit easy, you know."

"Vikram, don't fret. I believe in structured education and learning. I always grade my questions in ascending order of difficulty. If you know the answer, why don't you come out with it? Some people may get the wrong idea, you know, and think you are stalling for time. But not me. I am talking about—what did you say—yes, others of my ilk. Go ahead, answer the question."

Iti looked smug.

"In that case," said Vikram, flicking his hands in what he imagined was a gesture of careless abandon, "the answer is: a man, or a woman, for that matter."

"He is on his hands and knees during childhood and on his feet during his middle years. He walks with the help of a stick in the evening of his life and when he dies, four pall-bearers, that is, eight legs carry him to his funeral pyre."

The Brahmarakshas' grin broadened. When Iti spoke, his head moved up and down. When combined with his wide mouth, the sight was terrible to behold.

"You should know that I reserve my best for the last. I think my third question will be on some little-known aspects of old Indic grammar. I am afraid you will not be able to answer this question, as no one has done it so far."

"Wait, it is our turn to ask you a question."

Iti hesitated a little.

"You want to delay the inevitable? Fine. This will only give my appetite an edge."

Bana spoke up.

"As I understand it, if you are unable to answer the question we put to you or you give us an incorrect answer, you concede defeat and let us go. Right?"

"Well, it is a little worse than that for me. But, yes. I will have to let you go."

"Bana, you seem to have something on your mind. Do you have the right question for Iti?" Vikram queried.

"I have more than a perfect question to ask," said Bana *sotto voce.*

"Ask away, Bana," said Vikram.

Bana cleared his throat.

"Let me tell you a story," he began.

"Once upon a time, in the kingdom of Rajverma, in the town of Vidangan—"

"Get to the riddle already. Is all this germane?" Iti snarled.

Bana took one hurried look at Iti's face and paled.

"No, no the town was in...I see what you mean, want me to fast forward the story, right? Where was I? Forget the town and king. Father and son. Father marries a girl whose mother marries the son. The circumstances leading to it are interesting. Are you sure you don't want me to—okay, okay. You don't have to growl so. Anyway, in the fullness of time, a boy was born to the son and a girl to the father. The question is: what is the correct kinship relation between these children?"

Iti looked confused. Traces of fear began to show on its face. It began to think aloud.

"Let me take the boy child first and work out the relationship to the girl child's mother. That would be the boy child's father's father's wife. That would be the grandmother. Now, this is getting simpler. Wait, the girl child's mother is also the boy child's father's wife's daughter. Therefore, the girl child's mother is the boy child's sister. The sister is also his grandmother. Being his sister's grandson, he is also his own grand uncle. Therefore, the girl child's mother is his grand aunt..."

Iti's eyes had a mad look and spittle drooled down the corners of his mouth. Iti rambled.

"Therefore, the girl child's mother is his grand uncle's grand aunt. That would make her a great great aunt..."

He stopped abruptly.

"I don't know the answer. Please let me have the answer. This is killing me."

Bana spoke, "The terms and conditions clearly stipulate that if you do not know the answer, you let us go. There was no mention of our providing an answer. By the inviolable code of the Brahmarakshas, we demand that you let us go."

"I have to do more than that." Iti was looking miserable now. "This is what I have to do."

As they watched, Iti's body became elongated till it resembled a snake. It took its tail into its mouth and began to swallow itself.

In a short while, there was nothing but a concentrated glow of light where the Brahmarakshas had stood. A voice came from above: "Thank you for liberating me from the bearded one's curse. I am now free to continue my cycle of birth and rebirth. As a token of my appreciation, I will guide you out of this forest of doom into safety."

The luminescence started moving. Vikram and company got on their horses and followed it.

CHAPTER FOURTEEN

MAGIC

Vikram and his friends followed the glow through the forbidden forest. They concentrated on keeping it in sight. In their peripheral vision lurked dark shapes, pale figures, things that crawled, shadows that scooted and scurried, and forms that clomped and thundered. After trudging through the dense jungle for what appeared to be hours, they came to a fenced clearing.

Dwipada stood in front, with Ponni and Kamadenu behind.

The sphere of light flickered and coalesced into a shimmering, partly transparent human form.

"Iti, it's you! Why are you here? I thought I'd cursed you good and proper." Dwipada's face turned red as he spoke. As his anger grew, he began shouting, "I WILL CURSE YOU AGAIN!"

"Dwipada, Dwipada..."

The gentle rebuke in Bramara's voice brought Dwipada up short.

"Bramara...Bramarasena, *You!*"

"Don't you ever rest your third eye? Hush, Dwipada, for now. Besides, I don't want you to expend your *tapas* power unnecessarily."

Iti took advantage of the interlude. In a moment, Iti's form fragmented into multiple shards and faded rapidly.

Dwipada flashed a beatific smile at Bramara.

"Bramara, I notice you have changed. Or should I say, you have been forced to change your form?"

"Dwipada, I see that you are still your lovable bipolar self. I see that your feet are almost brushing the ground now. Anyway, we'll exchange compliments later. For now, I would like you to meet—"

"Vik, short for Vikram, Bana, short for Bana and Kalla, short for his age. And of course, Chetak," Dwipada preempted Bramara. "Don't look so amazed, Vikram," he continued. "I know the pasts, present and futures. By the way, the girl behind me is Ponni, not to be confused with the cow who is Gau—"

"MUUUU," Kamadenu bellowed.

"I mean, Kamadenu."

Vikram looked at Ponni and saw her glowering at him. His tattoo started to throb.

For a moment he was distracted by her large expressive eyes.

"Oh my God!" he burst out, "It's *you*. What are you doing here?"

"What are *you* doing here, Myself-Vikram-call-me-Vik?"

Vikram remembered and blushed.

"You are the last person I was hoping to meet. If I never see you again, it will be too soon."

"Children, please don't fight. There will be enough time for that later," said Dwipada as he ushered them all into the *ashram*. "In the meantime, there is lot of work to be done."

"Children?" muttered Vikram. "I am seventeen or I will be in a couple of months."

"And I am going to be four thousand. Give or take a hundred years," Dwipada said.

Vikram and Ponni walked stiffly alongside Dwipada, avoiding each other's eyes.

As they were walking back, Dwipada leaned towards Bramara. "Why don't you change into something more comfortable?"

"Not a bad idea. I see a cute parrot over there. Maybe I can have some fun." He changed into a parrot of five hues and flew away.

Vikram woke up feeling drugged. He heard the words: "Wake up, wake up! The sun has already risen." He saw Dwipada standing at the foot of his bed. A parrot, almost obscured by his beard, was perched on his shoulder.

"Is that you, Bramara?" asked Vikram, stifling a yawn.

"Of course it is me," said Bramara. "Can't you see I have worn a necklace to distinguish me from other parrots around here?"

"You look like a poitered garrot."

"What?"

"I mean a garroted potter. No, no! That isn't right either. You know, one of those parrots with a swollen neck."

"Arise, and if you can manage it, awake. You should blossom like a lotus bud encountering the first rays of the sun." Dwipada attempted to pull off Vikram's blanket.

"O sage, give me just a couple of minutes and I will see you outside." Vikram managed to hold on to the blanket. He splashed some cold water on his face from a mud pot and joined the others outside his cottage.

"I must say your face looks like a lotus that a war elephant has been toying with," Bramara said.

Vikram made a moue of distaste.

Bramara continued, "...one that has been dragged through mud and..."

Dwipada's beard trembled. He turned his head to one side and began to mutter. Vikram tried to listen in. After a few repetitions, the muttering became audible.

"I will keep my peace. I will not be a sage in a rage..."

It took a while for his beard to stop quivering. "If both of you are finished, I have something important to tell Vikram. Let us sit on these stones. No, not that one..."

Bramara settled himself on Vikram's shoulder. "Dwipada, what were you muttering?"

Dwipada looked embarrassed. "Well, nothing. It is just a mantra that Brahma taught me. He also gave me some advice after he bestowed the Chintamani jewel on me. Now that your curiosity is satisfied, can we have some seriousness?"

Bramara nodded.

Dwipada remained silent for a moment. When he spoke, his eyes shone like sparks from a fire stick.

"Vikram, you must understand that you are a child of destiny. All of us have a purpose in life. You have a very special one. You have been brought into this world for a specific purpose. You are the one chosen to put an end to the atrocities of Pisacha and liberate Orum from its isolation by bringing back the Chintamani."

Vikram was confused. "What? Who chose me? Why me? And what's a Chintamani? Why should I follow your agenda? I don't recall being consulted on this. In any case, how do you know that I am the one chosen?"

"*Shanti, shanti.* One question at a time. Chintamani is a magical stone that Pisacha stole from me. The magical power of Chintamani can and will be used to remove the force field around Orum. Why did someone choose you? In the larger scheme of things, the chooser, the chosen and the choice are one. I am not used to being questioned especially when the passive voice is used by me." He paused to mutter. "I won't be a sage in a rage, I won't be a sage in a rage, I won't be a sage in a rage."

Dwipada steadied himself, took hold of Vikram's hands and held them palms facing up.

"Look at the signs of the conch and the wheel. The ancient secret chronicles of the Gnomon speak of these symbols. At least they should because I certainly remember writing them down. You will also be well trained for this task. It is Bramara's job to train you—one of his purposes in life, if you will."

Bramara spoke, "Vikram, neither you nor I have a choice in this matter. You should learn to accept who you are."

Vikram thought of who he was—carefree as a newborn. He would jump into anything new with gusto, anything with a hint of adventure in it. Now, it seemed too many expectations were building up around him.

"I...I...feel so inadequate," Vikram said.

"Don't worry. You will learn. You are just beginning to mature. I can see a marked condensation of the magical field about you. With your enormous potential, you can achieve practically anything."

"You are saying all this because of a few lines on my hand? I always imagined that one of them actually looks like an owl and the other like an ostrich's egg."

"Vikram, the lines are only an indication of your potential. Let me show you what you can do, if you really put your mind to it."

"Do you see that large rock? Try to lift it without touching it."

"This huge rock here?" Vikram was doubtful.

"Lift!"

Vikram focused his will on the rock. Nothing happened.

"It is a myth," said Bramara, "that magic works because of a word and willpower. It's quite the reverse. It works because the magician knows that it will. It is faith rather than the will that moves mountains. Anything that can happen will happen if the power of absolute certainty is brought to bear."

"Sorry, I don't understand."

"Let me put it this way. Put aside your skepticism. Use your imagination. See the rock in your mind. Feel the texture. Smell it. Taste it. See it lift up. Feel it lift up. Be certain that the rock will move. Once it moves in your mind, it will do so in reality."

"I am not sure I have the imagination," said Vikram.

Dwipada closed his eyes for a moment.

"Of course you do. Do you remember, Vik, the time a teacher asked your class about an icosahedron?"

Vikram recalled the event.

It was a particularly long class and Vikram had drifted off into a world of his own. The question the teacher asked him, rather loudly, that brought him back to the classroom— "How many edges does an icosahedron with twenty faces and twelve vertices have?"

"Thirty," answered Vikram almost immediately.

"That was good. I am surprised you knew the formula. Class, the number of faces together with the number of vertices less the edges is always two."

"Apeechiko, I just turned the solid with twenty faces around in my mind and counted the edges."

"Very few people can picture such a solid in their minds and actually count the edges. You have always had a remarkable power of visualization. You have the power. Use it. Let it happen in the mind. It will happen in the real world."

Once again, Vikram closed his eyes and pictured the rock lifting up. To Vikram's astonishment, the rock rose with a whoosh and kept rising.

"Stop it, stop it," Dwipada cried out. The rock stopped in mid-air and started coming down, spinning slowly in the air.

"For a moment, I wondered how I was going to manage my washing," said Dwipada.

The instant the rock touched the ground there was a flash of light. In the place of the rock stood a short stocky man with a receding hairline and long braided hair. He joined his hands together in a gesture of respectful greeting. Vikram looked on in incredulity.

"Asadu! How is it...yes, I remember. I said the curse would be lifted when the stone is. Now what do I do with my washing? You know I would never use my dear beloved wife."

After a while, Dwipada's face cleared. "Yes, of course! Asadu, you can resume your duties as a disciple. Go to my cottage, collect the loincloths and upper clothes that need washing and take them to the river."

"Yes, master," said Asadu and left.

"Bramara," continued Dwipada, "carry on with Vikram's training. The next lunar eclipse is in a week. Pisacha will probably conduct his sacrifice on that day. Vikram and Ponni should be fairly prepared by then. We don't have much time. We meet at sundown at the sacrificial hall. Everybody needs to be there. We will discuss our strategy to rescue Jabala and others."

CHAPTER FIFTEEN

JABALA

Everything around Jabala wavered gently at first and then oscillated faster. Before it reached a crescendo, she closed her eyes, perhaps only for a second.

There was a roaring in her ears. Her eyes felt gritty and she wiped them with the back of her hand. She found sand in her hands and eyes. She opened her eyes fully. She was lying on a beach. The red pennant lay next to her, half buried in the sand, reminding her that she was the leader of the expedition.

The beach was dotted with the belongings of those in the procession—cloth bundles knotted expertly on top, anklets, bracelets, pearl necklaces, gauzy underwear, little containers of whitening powders and unguents, parchments, dried palm leaves, scribers and various oddments. The women were in different stages of waking up. Jabala's martial arts training came to her aid. She concentrated on her navel and let her awareness move up in degrees to her heart, to her throat and then to the space between her eyebrows.

She then jumped up, shook the sand out of her hair with a flick, pulled out the pennant from the sand and held it up. She found the whistle around her neck and blew three quick blasts into it.

When the all women had gathered around her, Jabala spoke.

"I am happy to see that all of us are fine. I don't know what has happened to my daughter. However, I hope she is in much less trouble than we are in. It is entirely possible that we have been kidnapped."

"I distinctly heard voices that said something like 'Pisacha Pinda'. We have to assume the worst, keep our wits about us and make the best of our current situation. I, like you, have absolutely no idea of where we are. We shall soon find out. Panicking will not help. I want you all to relax and center yourself as I have taught you."

"I can see the walls of a fort at a distance," said Madavi, whose height and grace were accentuated by twilight.

"I can see the walls of what appears to be a fort at a distance," continued Jabala, ignoring Madavi. "We are going there. I don't want us to arrive there as a bedraggled bunch. I would like you to get spruced up—powder your noses, oil and braid your hair, paint your eyes, moisten your lips, anoint your breasts with sandalwood paste—do whatever you have to do to be presentable. I will give you ten minutes. Your time starts now."

There was a flurry of activity around Jabala.

Soon, a group of twenty women were trudging toward the fort. As they approached it, they saw a drawbridge across a moat. Two men in full armor, holding broad-bladed scimitars, guarded the large gates. They remained motionless as the group crossed the bridge in a single file.

As Jabala approached, the gates swung open and the men continued to look straight ahead, faces expressionless. The women trooped in behind Jabala and stepped into the fort. The doors closed behind them.

They walked along the cobbled path toward the main building of the fort. Before they reached the entrance, a detachment of armed guards joined them. One of the guards, who was dressed a little differently with a peacock feather in his helmet, rode up to Jabala and spoke in a squeaky voice that belied his girth, "You are the leader of this expedition, aren't you? Come with me."

He swung to the left on a narrower path and kept pace with Jabala while the rest of them were corralled and herded on a direct course towards the main building.

"Where am I? Where are you taking me?" asked Jabala without expecting an answer.

"You are in Theevu. You are about to meet the *rakshasa* Trisiras." The guard grinned evilly.

The guard dismounted and blindfolded Jabala with a silken strip of cloth. They walked for a distance before they heard a grating, grinding noise, as though the earth had opened up.

"Watch your step," said the guard.

They went down steep steps. As they went down, the air smelt dank. A faint smell of burning oil permeated through the mustiness. There were no more steps; the ground continued to slope down. At last, they were on level ground. Jabala was allowed to remove her blindfold. She was now in a large underground cavern. The guard had disappeared. She could make out a stone throne on a raised platform with several steps. The arms and the back of the throne were adorned with stone skulls, which on closer examination resembled that of lions. Seated on the throne was a figure with...

"Finding my three heads fascinating, aren't you?"

A strange laughter followed. Jabala took some time to resolve the noise into 'hahaha,' 'hehehe' and 'hohoho' that were uttered simultaneously.

Despite the twinge of fear, Jabala felt her back stiffen. Her hands shook a little as she placed them on her hips.

"I guess three heads are better than one. I can't see you properly in this light."

Two spotlights came on and lit up Jabala and Trisiras.

"So, you are the leader of this group of virgins?"

For a moment Jabala was nonplussed at being addressed thus. She simply filed it away in her mind under 'For later'.

"Yes I am the leader. I am certified to lead groups. My name is Jabala. Are you Pisacha or...what's the name that minion mentioned—Trisiras?"

The two heads on either side swung forward to face Jabala. It was like an elephant flapping its ears. A single twisted horn rose from the top of his middle head. Three pairs of eyes focused on her. Did the eyes that beheld her soften or was it the effect of the lights? It was hard to say. A line of spittle snaked across the middle chin and dripped on to his hairy chest.

"I am Trisiras. Pisacha is my benefactor and friend. That is not important. You and your friends will be looked after well here... at least until the next lunar eclipse."

Again the three-toned laughter sounded.

"You will be given free rein to go anywhere on the island of Theevu at night. During the daytime, however, you will be confined to the fort. If any of you tries to escape, it will be the last time anybody hears of her. Or maybe, you will hear an agonized scream or two."

Concentrate. Get as much information as possible.

"What do you intend to do with us?"

Six eyes swung towards her again. Trisiras' inch-long sharp incisors were visible.

"You look delicious. Don't worry, I am not going to eat you. I don't eat humans anymore. Pisacha has weaned me of them. That's enough of talking. Now, be off with you. Go tell your friends all that I have told you." The spotlights faded and the guard appeared from nowhere.

She was blindfolded again.

They went back up the dank and smelly stairway. When they reached the top of the stairs, she heard the grinding noise again.

"Now that we are out of the tunnel," remarked Jabala, "why don't I take my blindfold off?"

"I suppose there is no harm," said the guard and untied the strip of cloth around Jabala's eyes.

She stood awhile till her eyes got accustomed to the light.

"You seem to be a smart young man," said Jabala, giving him a once-over.

"Actually, I am one of the oldest guards and the most senior officer here. I am the commander of the fort as well as captain of the elite guards." Jabala's eyes were busy noting the surroundings.

"There don't seem to be a lot of women here." Jabala looked coy.

"There aren't any. Well, there is one, a maid, but she doesn't come out often."

"Do you get a lot of visitors here?"

"We do get some once in a while, but they are all off before the next eclipse."

"Female visitors?"

"Yes, mostly females."

"That must keep you, er...occupied, right?"

"I have nothing to do with them. My religion forbids it, for now."

"For now?"

"Later, I have been promised 52 of them. True *rakshasis*. One per week."

"Have you ever tried to make out with a *rakshasi*? I mean, their feet don't touch the ground. They also point backwards. When you think they are making advances, they are actually retreating."

She waited expectantly for a reaction.

"That was a joke, wasn't it?"

"Yes."

"I thought as much. You couldn't have been serious. Surely you have heard of *rakshasi* beauties like Soorpanaka, Jrimbhika and Tataka."

"Why didn't you laugh then?"

"My religion forbids it. There is a saying, *'He who laughs last, laughs the most'*. I have also trained myself not to laugh, even under extreme provocation. I have trained with feathers and I keep getting some of the corpulent soldiers in my command to slip on banana peels. I never laugh. In any case, whatever expression I try on, it comes out as an evil grin."

"Are there a lot of people like you?"

Now the captain looked suspiciously at her.

"I am getting wise to you, lady. You are trying to pump me for information. If you talk anymore, I will be forced to tie this strip of cloth across your mouth."

They walked in silence after that.

When Jabala reached her allotted wing, her companions were busy settling in. Most were in the large hall. Some were in rooms abutting the hall. The one thing that stood out was the complete absence of windows. Trelliswork in the walls allowed in sunlight and air. The holes in the trellis were too small for one to put his head through.

A large number of rugs lay strewn around the hall. A table, which took up a large part of the room, had *rotis* heaped up on one of the trays and a bamboo basket containing an assortment of fruits. A big steaming tureen of fish curry stood in the center. A terracotta jug of water completed the fare.

Madavi went around the table a couple of times looking at the food from different angles. She finally declared, "The composition is stunning from here. Look at the light play on the fruit bowl. This is the angle from which I would like to paint it."

"You can paint it, if you wish to. You will have to do it later from memory. I am ravenous. I want to eat now," Jabala said.

There was very little talk after that, unless you count 'Pass the bread' or 'Leave some for me' as conversation.

Jabala spoke after they finished their meal. She first described her encounter with Trisiras. The discussion turned to their current situation and how they should cope.

"As I said earlier, we have been kidnapped by Pisacha and are now a prisoner of the *rakshasa* Trisiras. Any thoughts on why we have been brought here?" Jabala looked directly at Madavi.

Madavi was considered to be the one of the wisest of the lot, if not one of the most talented, despite being very young. Madavi cleared her throat. "I have heard of Pisacha from my father."

Her father was a magician of some renown at Akkam. He was regularly summoning recalcitrant demons and Madavi used to assist him by drawing the mystical diagrams for summoning them. She helped him interrogate them; the demons were usually fooled by her endearing looks. Madavi also learned to work some minor spells and helped her father write a book titled 'How to interrogate demons and keep the demon/yourself alive'.

One day, he simply disappeared, not in a multi-colored puff of smoke as demons or their tormentors do, but without a trace. Curiously enough, the attractive widow next door also disappeared around the same time. Madavi was brought up by her mother after that. "I have heard that Pisacha follows the left-hand path."

"Left-hand path?" Jabala's eyes narrowed.

"Black magic, aunty."

"Black Magic, did you say? And if you call me aunty again, I will spank you."

"Sorry, sorry. Bad path and evil magic. He is reputed to use human sacrifices for enhancing his magical powers. The important ones are conducted at the time of eclipses. I have heard that he uses virgin blood in his rites."

Another voice piped up: "Well, what for does he have us in here?"

There were a lot of giggles around the room, while some mothers looked suspiciously at their daughters.

Madavi continued, "There are expiatory acts that can be performed. For instance, if you can't get virgins, you break three coconuts for each..."

"That must take a lot of coconuts." The earlier speaker piped in.

There was laughter all around. The oppressive mood that pervaded earlier lifted. The discussion went on.

At last, Jabala stood up and summarized.

"One. We will keep our eyes and ears open. We will also try and get as much information as possible from the people who work here.

"Two. It is more than possible that Pisacha is going to have us sacrificed, perhaps, at the next lunar eclipse as Madavi suspects. The next one is just two weeks away. We do not have much time. We must escape by then.

"Three. Knowing my daughter Ponni, she will make an attempt to find and rescue us. We must gather enough information about the layout of this place from the guards who are posted here and around Trisiras. Madavi, you are the resident artist. You will make a map of the island and the fort. When we know more, we will firm up our plans. Meanwhile, all of us will have to keep fit. Every morning, we will gather here. I will lead you through basic physical and martial arts training."

CHAPTER SIXTEEN
GANDA BERANDA

It was the fourth day of their captivity. Madavi finished making a map of the island. She also befriended Trijada, a maid who brought them food and whom she was hypnotizing in degrees.

Madavi and Jabala sat on the beach. The young girl was gazing at the waves and the sky while Jabala stared curiously at a floating piece of seaweed.

"Interesting, there are floating seaweeds here. Did you know seaweed is effective in treating consumption?"

An image of eating mountains of seaweed to cure overeating flashed across Madavi's mental eye.

"Are they slimming, Aun...Jabala?"

"I am not sure, but the disease is."

"The disease?"

"Yes, consumption wastes away your flesh and you start losing weight."

Madavi's face cleared.

"Oh...how do you know so much about diseases, plants and medicinal herbs, Aun...er, Jabala?" Madavi asked with her gaze still on the sea.

"Oh, one of my...um...husbands was a doctor and a naturalist."

Madavi was staring at something at a distance in the sky. There seemed to be a hint of rain in the sky except that the thunderclouds seemed to be moving too fast for there to be any sustained downpour.

An indistinct form, which first appeared to be a cloud, grew bigger as it neared the fort. She could soon make out the form of a bird with long sharp talons and two heads. Its bronze feathers glinted in the sunlight. From where they were seated, they could see two of the towers projecting up from the defensive walls of the fort. The huge bird was heading towards the southwestern tower of the fort.

"A Ganda Beranda!" Madavi exclaimed.

Seeing the blank expression on Jabala's face, she continued, "I have never seen one before. I have only heard about them. Their favorite prey is the elephant but the hungry ones will eat anything. Reputedly, they are the strongest beasts on land and in air."

The Ganda Beranda went into a screaming dive, aiming for the top of the tower. Several arrows from the tower struck the bird and glanced off without penetrating. In an instant, the giant bird was at the tower. Soon, it emerged from inside. It had two squirming guards in each of its beaks and two goats held carelessly in its talons. The bird now soared high up.

An arrow shot from the tower struck close to a leg of the Ganda Branda and it dropped one of the guards. The guard came down screaming, spread-eagled and spinning through the air. He fell into the ocean with a splash.

The goats and the other guard disappeared in a flash. Only a slight chewing motion of the beaks remained. The bird stopped chewing and gathered itself for another dive, this time towards the northwestern tower.

Suddenly, a sound of triple laughter rent the air. This time the pitch was many notches higher. It was the closest Jabala ever came to shuddering.

Trisiras jumped over the wall and stood directly beneath the tower.

"EAT MY GOATS, GANDA?" he thundered and launched himself at the diving bird. Beast and *rakshasa* met in mid-air. Feathers flew. Trisiras let go of Ganda and watched it spiral down in deep distress.

After a while, Trisiras dived after the Ganda. This time, the *rakshasa's* massive hand reached for a neck. "This is the head that ate my goat, right?" he asked as he squeezed it. In a few moments, the head hung limp. He let go and vaulted back over the wall.

Laughter echoed as the Beranda's careening flight took it away from the island.

"That was a display of raw power. Do you think the Ganda lost because he dropped his guard?"

Jabala was too preoccupied to reply.

Trijada, so fair she almost appeared pale, entered the hall, dragging a food trolley behind her.

Madavi sat alone.

"Why don't you help me lay...?"

"*Choo mandarakkali,*" said Madavi.

You cannot be hypnotized against your will unless you believe in hypnotism. The trick in hypnotizing someone is to first make them believe in it. This is what Madavi had achieved with Trijada as a first step. On that day, she decided to test how well her trigger word worked with Trijada.

Trijada's demeanor changed. Her eyes glazed over. Her shoulders stiffened. She froze and stared ahead.

"You are ready to spill the beans now," observed Madavi.

Trijada reached into the food trolley, found the mud pot with the bean salad, lifted it high over her head and smashed it to the ground.

Hearing the sound, Jabala came out of her room and into the hall. She took one look at Trijada's rigid stance, looked at Madavi and raised a questioning eyebrow. Madavi nodded.

"You will now go back in time. What is your name? What do you do?" Jabala queried.

"I am Aparanji. I have a lot of fun doing my job. I entertain people by dancing at the temple and..."

"I must have made some mistake," whispered Madavi. "I seem to have regressed her right into a past life."

Madavi looked at Jabala, who nodded at her to continue.

"Come back to your current birth. You are Trijada now."

"I am Trijada.""Who do you work for?"

"Trisiras."

"Who or what is he?"

"Trisiras told me he was once a mighty *asura*, who was considered to be one of the up-and-coming demons in hell. One day, when the other *asuras* were busy churning the ocean of milk, their *guru* Sukra found him goofing off with a cup of wine in his hand. The angry *guru* banished him from the seven hells. He roamed the earth for eons, living off the land, eating anything and everything until he met Pisacha, for whom he now works. Pisacha gave him a place to stay and a plentiful supply of goats. In return, Trisiras guards Theevu."

"Do you know where he is quartered?"

"Yes, he lives in his underground chamber. I go there every day to top up his wine cask. There is a secret underground passage that leads out from the fort grounds. The door to the passage opens only when I say the magic words."

"Open Sesame?"

Trijada seemed to hesitate a little. "Yes," she admitted.

"Have you talked to him recently? What did he say, for instance, when you saw him last?"

"I met him last night. When I went in to refill the wine cask, I found it empty. He did not talk much. There were dozens of tarantulas on the ground, most of which seemed dead. He was holding a giant spider in his hands and pulling off its legs one by one, all the while muttering 'Jabala loves me' alternating it with 'Jabala loves me not'. He was obviously getting frustrated and angry."

Madavi looked at Jabala significantly. Jabala raised a thoughtful eyebrow.

"What did you do next?"

"I suggested that, on the next tarantula, he start with 'Jabala loves me not'. I then ran back to my quarters."

"How can Trisiras be killed?"

"He cannot be killed."

"Why do you say that? Is he immortal?"

"One day, when he was drunk, he told me that his life force does not reside inside his body. It lies hidden in a place known only to him."

"I am now getting a handle on this. I have an idea." Jabala said in a low tone. "You can terminate the interrogation now."

"*Choo mandrakkali,*" said Madavi.

Later, the two women were back in their room. Madavi looked forlorn.

"Oh, what's the use?" Madavi wailed. "He is simply too strong. Look at the way he toyed with the Ganda Beranda. We can't escape until we kill him. To kill him is next to impossible. Therefore..."

"Madavi, don't be so negative. Where there is a will there may be a way. There may be a hidden codicil, for instance. Every cloud has a silver lining."

"But this one doesn't even have enough to coat half a sweet."

"Stop that, Madavi. The drawings of the island and the fort are almost ready. We need one last piece of information to make our plan. We have to find out the location of Trisiras's life force."

"And do you have any bright ideas? I suppose you could go and ask him."

"Yes, that is exactly what I plan to do."

"What? Jabala, you must be out of your mind!"

"No, listen to me."

For the next half hour, Jabala elaborated on a plan that had been brewing in her mind.

Madavi's face cleared. "Yes, this could work," she said, almost to herself. "We have it from a reliable source that he is sweet on you. I will arrange for some art materials and get to work."

CHAPTER SEVENTEEN

BRAMARA IS AWAY

Vikram was seated in the sacrificial hall with Bramara perched on his shoulder. Bramara seemed to like his parrot form so much that he hadn't changed into anything else. Kalla and Bana sat next to him. Ponni sat across from him but kept her face averted. The aroma of the previous day's *homa*, combined with that of the cow dung with which the floor was purified, pervaded the hall. Dwipada's beard entered first, followed by Dwipada and Asadu. He sat facing the group and looked straight into Vikram's eyes.

"We have to find where Pisacha has taken the people in the procession and rescue them."

"I thought you knew the pasts."

"Who said that?" Dwipada looked around. He detected the movement of an equine shadow behind an open window.

"Chetak, you won't understand, which is why you are not a part of the meeting. The pasts are innumerable and vast. They are accessible to me only at a very large-grained level. This particular event seems to be at the grain boundaries. In any case, some parts of the future are clear. For instance, I can see your upper teeth growing so long that they will pierce your jaw and prevent you from talking. I can also see that you are going to play a leading part in a horse sacrifice. Now, will you get lost and go look for yourself?"

"Is that a curse, O Venerable Seer?" Chetak's voice could be heard from behind the wall.

"It is a prediction—one that is waiting to become a curse."

Chetak's shadow disappeared from the window in a hurry.

Bramara spoke. "The lad will be ready in three weeks. He has a lot of hidden potential."

"Mostly hidden," he added in a low voice.

"What did you say, Bramara? Can you speak clearly and not squawk? Asadu, get me my hearing aid."

"Nothing of importance, Dwipada."

Asadu brought him his hearing aid, which was made of dried leaves stitched together with bits of pine needles and shaped into a cone.

Ponni sat with her chin resting on her hands.

"Anyway, why should Vikram do anything? What is in it for him?" she asked.

Vikram looked offended.

Bramara looked sly, if it were possible for a parrot to look so.

"Vikram will merely be performing the duties of a son-in-law." He saw fiery darts emanating from Vikram's eyes and added hastily, "—to-be."

"That stupid *swayamvaram* ceremony means nothing. I wish I could get rid of these." Ponni rubbed her tattoo as she said this.

"Hey, don't think I was very happy with all that either. Anyway, you chose me in a proper *swayamvaram*." Vikram retorted.

"Yes. And what choice did I have?" She pointed to Vikram's friends seated next to him, with a sweep of her arm. "These?"

Kalla started to protest. Bramara shushed him.

"No fighting. Let us take it for granted that Vikram and his friends will do their best. Let us move on."

Dwipada turned towards Ponni. "Do you remember anything that will help us? You were there when Jabala and others disappeared."

Ponni's expression turned serious. "I saw a flash and heard a bang. I heard voices shouting 'Victory to Pisacha Pinda'."

"Pisacha!" Dwipada exclaimed. "That confirms it."

There was a new sense of urgency in Dwipada's voice. "It is vital that we rescue the women at once. And not just for their sakes."

"They could have been whisked away to any place on the earth. Where do we begin searching for them?" asked Asadu.

"I have an idea," Bramara said. "Can you lead me to the place where this occurred?"

"The whole scene is clear in my mind. Why do you ask?" Ponni looked animated.

"Magical fields affect everything around them. The intensity of the field required to teleport such a large group must have been very high. The field enveloping them would have left a telltale trace along the way. In my bee form, I can detect strong magic. I may be able to follow the trail all the way to where they were taken."

"That is settled," Dwipada said. "Ponni, you will go with Bramara to the spot where Jabala and others were abducted. You will then return. Bramara will follow the trail, find where they are taken, meet them if possible and report back to me. We will then make plans for their rescue."

Ponni set off at a brisk pace. Bramara settled himself comfortably on Ponni's shoulders. She walked quietly for a while.

"I was just wondering..." said Bramara. Ponni glanced up.

"...whether you are a little sweet on that boy."

"What on earth are you talking about, Polly?"

"The boy, Vikram, and the name is Bramara. You just pretend to fight with him, don't you?"

Ponni felt blood rush to her cheeks.

"What are you now? Some kind of a counselor? Or are you one of those birds that hang around lovelorn maidens as though they were bosom companions. And even..." Ponni shuddered. "...sing songs to them about milk being sour, the cool breeze burning them up and so on, just because the lover has taken a bathroom break?"

"Come, come, Ponni. Tell me truly, hand on your heart, that you don't like Vikram at all."

"What if I do and what is it to you?"

"I am a well-wisher. Now tell me truly because the boy is hopelessly in love with you. He has been talking about nothing else but your lovely big eyes and the dimples that form on your cheek when you smile. I have seen him glance at you, when you are not looking, and sigh like a *yali* in heat."

"Vikram. He cannot sigh even if you pumped him full of gas and poked him with a red-hot needle. In fact, when I have—" she stopped abruptly.

"Ha, just as I suspected. You have been making eyes at him, right?"

Ponni saw Bramara's eyes distracted by a movement on one of the lower branches of a willow tree. A bird was perched on the tree with its head cocked to one side. A signal passed between Bramara and the other parrot. Before Ponni could say, "Wow, that's a cute looking bird," Bramara flew off, joined the bird and the two vanished.

Ponni continued walking on without further incident and reached the place where she had seen the *nagas*. Bramara returned just as Ponni reached the spot. He seemed disheveled and happy. One of his tail feathers now adorned his head.

"You look like a parrot with terminal Psittacosis," Ponni remarked, "You must have had fun with that parrot."

"That was not a parrot but a common wench. Anyway, never mind, just tell me if this is the place."

"Yes, we were coming along the trail here..."

She pointed to the trail with an expansive gesture. Her hand stopped in mid-air and jerked back a little.

"That is the energy field surrounding Orum." Bramara changed into his original bee form.

"I can now smell the aftermath of an intense black magic field. I can follow this spoor. I just will change back into a bird and Babu is your uncle."

"No, Babu is my cousin. Although, since he married my aunt…" Ponni was lost in thought.

"No time to waste. I will be on my way." Bramara changed back into a parrot and was poised for flight.

"Wait," cried Ponni, coming out of her musings. "I know my mother. If you meet my mother and her friends, how will you prove that you are one of the good guys? Or my envoy? If she doesn't believe you are who you say you are, you will become a pot of parrot curry in no time. I have an idea. Take this."

She untied a knot on her sari, took out a brooch with a large stone set in it and held it out to Bramara.

"What's this? What do I do with it? Bribe your mother?"

"Don't be silly, Polly. This is a brooch that my mother presented me on my tenth birthday. It is a priceless jewel. It's set with a rare ten-carat diamond. At least that's what she said. This wasn't true, I found that out when I tried to flog it last year. The pawnbroker said this was a worthless paste. I haven't told my mother that I know. Anyway, she'll be able to identify this as mine. This will be evidence that you are carrying my message."

"Such a large brooch! What do I do with it? Where do I put it?"

"Don't worry. I won't look." Ponni turned around, facing away from the parrot.

When she looked back a few minutes later, Bramara was gone.

CHAPTER EIGHTEEN

TRISIRAS

Jabala looked at the portrait from various angles. Finally, she nodded. "Looks good. Though I appear younger and far more...endowed. The lotus I am holding out is realistic. Madavi, you have done a great job. Do you think you can handle the rest?"

"Handle it? Ha. I can enchant pictures blindfolded. In a dark room. At twenty paces. On a moonless night. In fact—"

"I get it. Now, just go ahead and do it."

Madavi's face was tight with concentration. A beam of light shot out from her hands and touched the lotus in the picture. For a moment, the entire picture was suffused with a pink radiance. Then it faded, leaving behind a subtle after-glow on the flower.

Jabala quickly threw a cloth over the picture.

"Let's summon Trijada now."

Jabala's voice held a note of satisfaction.

"*Choo mandrakkali*," uttered Madavi as soon as Trijada entered. She wasted no time in giving her instructions.

"You will see to it that Trisiras is kept plied with wine through the day. In the evening you will take this picture to his room and ask him to look at it. Make sure that you don't look at the picture before he does."

"He will probably behave strangely once he sees it. Come back and report to us. *Choo mandarakkali.*"

Trijada carried the picture draped in a cloth along with a third refill of the wine cask. At Trisiras's den, she found three mugs of wine on the rough-hewn stone table and an empty cask. Trisiras was bent over one of the mugs. All his brows were creased. It was clear that he was thinking.

Trijada rested the picture on the wall in front of him, whipped off the cloth and said, "Sire, take a look at this."

Trisiras looked up and the effect on him was startling. His eyes seemed to pop out of their sockets. He scrambled across the room to get closer to the picture. Two of his tongues were hanging out. He went down on his knees.

"Fair fair fair maiden maiden maiden, give me the flower," he said. The wine had obviously caused a bit of lag in his normally synchronized speech. As Trijada left the room, she could still hear him repeating over and over again, 'Fair maiden, give me the flower'.

Jabala took extra care over her appearance. She washed her face with turmeric and her eyes with collyrium. She then applied kohl generously to her eyes and some splashed *attar* on her pulse points. She chewed betel with quicklime to get the desired red coloration to her lips and tongue. She braided her hair with *champaka* flowers. The silk sari she wore was generously worked with gold thread. She wore a pearl necklace, a girdle of gold and anklets that produced a musical sound when she walked. She carried a basket of jasmine flowers.

Along with Trijada, she had already reconnoitered the entrance to the underground den. When she entered Trisiras's room, the *rakshasa* was still on his knees in front of the portrait, entreating the woman in it to part with the flower in her hand.

Trisiras looked up at the sound of Jabala's anklets. He rubbed two of his eyes in apparent disbelief.

"Yes, I am the real one, my life-master," she said.

Trisiras got up, stumbled and regained his balance.

"Did you just call me your life-master?" he asked.

"Yes, and I also meant to call you my piece of jaggery."

"The love of my life, my very existence," he said and caught her in a tight embrace and showered fiery kisses on her forehead, lips and chin, while another tongue snaked deep into her mouth. Or so he would have, if he had read *The Fragrant Lawn—Or what the Gnomons don't teach you*. He hadn't, so he didn't. Instead, he squirmed slightly.

"Do you really mean it?" he asked.

"Yes, I do. However our love must remain unfulfilled..."

Jabala paused a little and sighed deeply and audibly.

"Why? Is there someone else that you like? Tell me who it is and I will eat him up. Then, not only will that person be out of the way, I would also have gained the qualities you like by eating him."

"No, no. It is because I am afraid. Very afraid." Again she wanted to pause but was worried that Trisiras would fill up the gap by saying something. She settled for a beat. "I am afraid that what I love will end up dying. When I was young, I had a mayfly as a pet. I still remember the day it died. Come to think of it, that was the day I found it and put it in a matchbox."

"Don't worry. Stick with me and I will catch you two mayflies everyday."

"You mistake me. I am worried about you. True, you are big and strong and have a way with Ganda Beranda birds. What if you should..."

She turned away from him, put an arm over her eyes and whispered with a realistic catch in her throat. "...die?"

Jabala was startled when she heard the signature laugh. It took Trisiras a while to wipe the tears of mirth from all his eyes.

"Die, *die*, DIE? Not while my life force is safe inside a bee in the sacred grove."

"A bee! How wonderful, darling! That means that you are safe. Unless..."

The fountain of Jabala's gushing switched off abruptly.

"Oh my gods, I know what bees are like. They flit. Repeatedly. From flower to flower. What if it flies away and is caught by some awful bee eater?"

"Don't you worry your little heads, I mean head. It's inside a box."

"That's a great piece of news. I am happy or rather will be happy if it is in a place where no one can find it easily."

"It is hidden in one of the upper branches of a *peepul* tree in a grove. Even if someone discovers it, he will have to find the key to the box."

Jabala stamped her feet. "Just tell me the whole thing, will you? Where is the key to the box? Getting information from you is like pulling teeth..."

The irritation in Jabala's voice got through to Trisiras. He hastened his replies.

"Key inside golden lotus deep inside pond."

"And I reckon the tree will be difficult to identify..."

"Well, it is marked with a red trident at its base. But you have to know that to be able to look for it, right?"

Right you are.

There was still one more piece of information that she needed.

I cannot get him suspicious.

"I am so relieved, my jackfruit-dipped-in-honey. I can start my Gauri vow."

"Good, good. I will just clear that heap of goat bones over there and you and me..."

"You didn't hear me, Tri. My vow means I cannot be with any man for seven days. You too will have to follow certain rituals."

"You will have to offer flowers to the goddess Gauri every day. For this to be effective, it has to done without fail every day."

"Every day?" Trisiras said, in a daze.

"Take this flower basket. One flower today. Four tomorrow. Sixteen the next day. Four times that the following day. When you run out of flowers, ask your guards to get you more."

"Twenty, sorry, sixty-four," said Trisiras after what seemed an eternity. His brows were knit in concentration and his lips were moving.

"That's right. And so on till the end of the vow."

"I hope I can keep seeing you meanwhile."

"Just concentrate." Jabala's annoyance was showing through now. "Let me test you. What do you do when you run out of flowers?"

"That's easy. I run out to you and ask for more." Trisiras looked smug. He had the look of someone who had said something clever and original.

"NO," Jabala almost shrieked. "You ask your guards to gather them for you. Got it?"

"Yes, yes, of course," said Trisiras. "I ask the guards. But when do I get to see you?"

"Not until the end of my vow."

"Why not?"

"I can't trust myself to keep pure in your irresistible presence..."

Her eyes were drawn to the mass of lichen on his exposed navel.

"Your lich... I mean likable countenance—countenances. I know it is going to be incredibly hard for me not to see you for seven days and likewise for you. In fact, that is why I sent you my picture. You can...er... offer flowers to it. Hard as it is, this is not what I am worried about." A beat. "My love," she continued. "Promise me something..."

"Promise," said Trisiras.

"You won't think I worry too much if I am still worried about something?"

Before Trisiras could speak, she continued.

"What if..."

Her voice broke and mended magically.

"What if someone enters that grove and you can't get there in time because it is too far?"

In reply, Trisiras strode to one of the walls of his room. "Open Sesame," he shouted.

A hole appeared in the wall. He gestured expansively.

"This leads to the grove, which is right outside the fort walls"

Done.

Jabala exulted.

CHAPTER NINETEEN

BRAMARA AT THEEVU

Bramara followed the stench of black magic quite easily, even in his bird form. It led him over the sea; the long flight left him tired. Just as he was wondering whether he should change into a seagull, he saw an island that gleamed golden in the rays of the rising sun. A fort dominated the landscape. He flew around the island to memorize its orientation and features. The island was roughly pentagonal, an apex pointing due north, the ground sloping up sharply to the south and falling away precipitously at the other end of the fort. A large fenced pasture nestled at its northwest corner. A long, low-roofed building hugged the ground at the southeast corner. He made a mental note.

Bramara flew over the fort and alighted on to a large courtyard. Two women were busy in conversation. He thought he was behind their line of vision and therefore unobserved.

He cocked his head to one side and looked at their feet to ensure that these were not *rakshasis*. The feet were firmly planted on the ground and pointing forward. Bramara was sure that these were women from the procession. He hopped towards them and opened his beak...

...only to find himself struggling in the grip of a small-made woman. "Your colors are far too vivid for you to be an ordinary parrot. I would like to know why you were looking at our legs." The musical voice belied her strength, as did her appearance.

"Squawk!" said Bramara and corrected himself hastily by squawking.

There was something familiar about the woman's appearance.

She is an older version of Ponni.

"You are Jabala, Ponni's mother, aren't you? Let me go. I have traveled far to meet you."

"He looks so sweet. Do let him go," said Madavi. Her cheeks dimpled.

"You will stay within my reach. You try and escape...you will be the main ingredient of a parrot curry." Jabala's grip relaxed. It took some time for Bramara to recover his breath.

"Ponni did warn me about your culinary skills," said Bramara.

"Tell me who you are and how you know my daughter."

Bramara related the story of how Ponni had stumbled into Dwipada's *ashram* and how he was charged with reconnoitering and getting a message across to Jabala.

Jabala listened with rapt attention.

"That still doesn't tell me who you are," said Jabala, steel entering her voice.

"That is not important. For the present, I am a well-wisher. However, I can prove to you that I am an envoy of your daughter."

Bramara flew into the bushes behind them and when he emerged, he held out the brooch that Ponni had given him. Jabala looked at it and her face cleared.

"This is the paste...I mean, invaluable brooch that I'd given my daughter. I am sorry for doubting you, Meenakshi—"

"My name is not Meenakshi. I am a male parrot. Look at the coloring just above my beak. And I am not Mittoo. I am not Ranga. My name is Bramara. Short for Bramara Sena."

"Got it. Thanks a lot. What is the plan for the rescue?"

"Before we decide on a plan, we need to gauge the strength of the enemy. We have to find out how many guards there are and how they are deployed."

"We have already done our homework. I think we have gathered enough intelligence."

Madavi went on to describe the island, the layout of the fort and the guard detail.

"There is, however, one crucial factor. This island is governed by Trisiras, a *rakshasa* with immense strength. He is virtually undefeatable."

She then narrated the encounter with the Ganda Beranda and described at length where the *rakshasa's* life force lay, detailing the underground passages that linked Trisiras' den to various places.

"There is a link from his room to the grove where his life force is stored. There must be another tunnel from outside the fort. Every day, fifty goats are taken into the building at the southeast end of the island. Sometimes, some skeletons are taken out. No live goat has ever been seen to come out. There must be a tunnel linking Trisiras to his food supply."

"This is Madavi's handiwork." Jabala said as Madavi handed over a map of the fort and the island.

"Did you just wink at me?" Madavi enquired.

Bramara was busy poring over the map.

"The problem is that there are just too many guards both inside and outside the fort," said Bramara, looking up.

"I think we can disable the guards inside the fort, if you warn us in advance. I have ensured that the guards outside will be busy otherwise. When you come with help, just stay away from the large garden on the western portion of the island—that's the one with a lot of flowering trees."

Bramara's voice showed respect for Jabala. "We will return as soon as possible. In all probability, I will come ahead of the others and let you know what our plans are. You will definitely have to play a major role."

Bramara then took off.

"The map," shouted Madavi, "you left behind the map."

"I know," muttered Bramara as he flew away without a backward glance.

"That is an excellent map, Madavi," said Jabala.

"Thank you. I hope this helps us."

Jabala's eyes were narrowed in thought.

"You have marked a lily pond on the map. Where there are lilies, there are frogs. Did you see any in the pond?"

"Oh yes, I saw some beautiful golden frogs."

"How big were they?"

"Large, as frogs go."

"Just as I thought," said Jabala with obvious satisfaction in her voice.

"Here is what you do. Catch some of those frogs. All of them, if you can. On no account should you touch them. Use a ladle. Put them in a water pot. Scrub their skins with a brush. Keep the wash carefully. Take the frogs and put them back into the pond. In a couple of days, most of the wash-water would have evaporated, leaving behind what we want."

Jabala made Madavi repeat the instructions.

CHAPTER TWENTY
INTELLIGENCE

Ponni looked critically at the wooden bird, a target that Asadu had set amidst the branches of a tree. Asadu measured two hundred paces from the target and studied it from that distance. He nodded to himself with satisfaction. He handed a long bow and a quiver of arrows to Ponni, who slung it over her left shoulder.

"What do you see?" asked Asadu.

"I see only the eye of the bird," replied Ponni.

Asadu's face fell. "Don't steal my lines. Let me ask again. What do you see?"

"I see the tree, the branches and the bird on it."

"That's better. Rather, that is not what you should see. You must be focused entirely on the eye. The target should fill your sight, mind, your entire being."

"That is what I said..."

"Now hold the bow up and pull back the string toward you such that your hand brushes gently against your right ear."

"I can't do it," said Ponni.

"Why not...oh my god. You are left-handed. Make it the left ear."

"Now," he continued, "let the arrow go. Let it release you rather than you releasing it."

Ponni turned to him with a puzzled look.

"Let me put it this way. Have you ever had diarrhea?"

The arrow sped from her bow. The wooden bird fell from the branch. Both went to retrieve the target. Ponni saw that the arrow had fallen near the target.

"I was hoping the arrow would have been stuck in the eye," said Ponni, picking up the target.

"I put a glass eye on the target," said Asadu.

"What a mean trick!" exclaimed Ponni.

"It just makes it reusable." Asadu shrugged as he put the target back on a branch. "Not a bad shot at all."

"For a woman, I mean," he added hastily.

Ponni's expression turned bleak.

"I have trained since I was four and I am the current state champion for blindfold shooting in all of Akkam and Bakkam. The contests involve shooting at vegetables and fruits placed atop people's heads."

"Live people?" asked Asadu, incredulity showing in his tone.

"Yes, at least before the shot."

"Sorry for underestimating you," said Asadu, respect creeping into his voice. "And you shoot blindfolded."

"You mistake me," said Ponni, "It's the potential victims who are blindfolded. Anyway, they are chosen from prisoners jailed for violent crimes."

"I was wondering," mused Ponni as they walked back, "how you became a master of archery. Pardon me for asking, but haven't you spent most of your life as a washing stone?"

Asadu waited a little before responding. "I was born with this ability. My master explained it to me."

Ponni made encouraging noises.

Asadu continued. "I was a hunter in my last birth. One of the mightiest the land had ever seen. I was so good that I could hear a sound and shoot accurately at the source of that sound, even without actually sighting the target. Once I heard a rustling in the middle of the forest and shot at it. When I went near, I found that I had shot a male deer, which had been...er...sporting with a female deer."

"The female deer ran away but the male deer turned into a sage—an angry one with an arrow in the middle of his chest. The sage cursed me to be cursed in my next birth. He then said something even more alarming. 'Your next birth begins now'. I fell down dead. I was reborn with the same amazing skills at archery."

"It still does not explain why you were such a skilled archer in your last birth."

"Oh. My master explained that too; in fact, he took me through that. In my birth before that..."

Ponni was happy that a scream interrupted their conversation.

The screeching noise was from a parrot with a hawk in hot pursuit.

Ponni nocked an arrow, drew the bowstring and let go.

The hawk veered away from pursuit with half its tail feathers missing.

"Not bad shooting, huh...for a woman, I mean," said Ponni.

"You needn't have...done it. I was only...teasing the hawk," said Bramara, breathing hard as he landed.

Ponni was the last to walk into the meeting. The hall had been cleaned. Mattresses were placed all around. Fresh sand lay in a heap in one corner. Kalla and Vikram sat together. Dwipada, Bramara and Asadu were seated together as a group. Bana sat by himself with palm leaves to take notes.

Bramara looked unruffled as he took center stage.

"We were waiting for you," Bramara said.

"Did you find my mother?" Ponni asked, impatience showing on her face.

"Yes, of course. She's fine. I didn't have to go about gathering information. She had it all ready for me."

Bramara went on to describe the location of the island, the fort on the promontory and the guards. After that, he busied himself drawing a map of Theevu and its fort on the sand bed.

"I suppose, you must have met Madavi too," asked Kalla almost nonchalantly.

"Madavi...hmm...let me see, Madavi. Isn't that the pretty girl with a straight back? Tall girl. Must be taller than you." Kalla reddened.

"One with dimples on both cheeks?"

"Yes, yes," said Kalla.

"I am not sure I saw anyone like that," said Bramara. "There was this one other girl who had gathered a lot of intelligence. Resourceful girl, that." Kalla looked crestfallen.

"The main problem will be in reaching the island." Dwipada's beard showed signs of agitation.

"We should get hold of a large boat to take us there." Ponni was getting impatient.

"I wish we could fly into the island," said Vikram.

"Yes, we could use an airplane," said Dwipada. "I forget. Airplanes haven't been invented yet."

"I wish Bramara was as big as a *yali*," said Kalla. "Then he could carry us all."

Dwipada's eyes shone. "That's it. You've got it," exclaimed Dwipada. "We will use *yalis*."

"Why would a *yali* want to carry us when she would rather eat us?" Vikram looked puzzled.

"A *yali* gave you her feather. That is a token of her obligation to help you. You did lead the *yalis* to their arch enemies, the *nagas*."

Ponni felt a frisson of fear and excitement at the same time.

"There is still the problem of Trisiras. He simply cannot be defeated in a one-on-one combat." Bramara looked up from the diagram he was creating with much exertion of beak and talon.

"However," he continued, "Jabala has been able to learn the location of the *rakshasa's* life-essence. It is inside a bee in a box that can be opened by a key, which is inside a lotus in a pond. The box is on one of the top branches of a large tree in a grove. The grove is just outside the fort walls."

I knew my mother would do it.

"Then all we have to do is get into the grove and crush that bee," summarized Ponni.

"There's a catch though," said Bramara. "The grove is heavily guarded by a team of elite soldiers who have all taken a terrible oath—they are sworn to die protecting Trisiras. They apparently took the oath placing their right hand on their mothers' heads, in some cases, their dead mother's skulls."

"That's some oath!" said Vikram.

"Sacred and inviolable," said Dwipada.

"That's not what I meant," said Vikram.

"But there is another way into the grove," continued Bramara, "That's through the *rakshasa's* den. That is what we have to use. Jabala said she could figure out a way to get past Trisiras. Luckily, she has been able to get close to him. Then there is the problem of getting twenty women out."

"Do we really need to?" said Kalla in an aside to Vikram. "You know, two of them are our mothers-in-law-to-be."

Seeing the expression on Ponni's face, he quickly added, "I was only joking."

"It certainly won't be possible to ride on a *yali*," said Dwipada. "You can't have more than two people on her back. Sure, she is strong but her body bits will interfere if there are more than two people on her back. Also, there won't be more than four *yalis* since they hang out in quadriads."

"Can't they carry a stick? The women can hang by their teeth. Quite like the story my mother read out..."

Normally, whenever Bana went into his creative excursions, a chorus of 'Will you shut up?' greeted him.

This time it was different.

"That gives me an idea," Dwipada said. He looked at Bana and cleared his throat.

Asadu knew that it was a prelude to a story and groaned.

"You wanted to say something, Asadu?" Dwipada's voice was level.

"No, Master. I just have this pain in my throat."

"I will give you an herbal extract. A really bitter one. You might throw up several times after that but it will cure your pain."

Dwipada cleared his throat again. Asadu kept quiet.

"I will tell you a story," he began, keeping his eyes firmly fixed on Asadu while nodding encouragingly at Bana who was writing furiously.

"There was this hunter, a mighty hunter by the name Ekalavya. He once decided to ensnare a large flock of parrots that used to frequent a weeping walnut tree. He worked hard for years and in the end, he had the biggest and the strongest net snare ever made. It was woven out of the silk of giant spiders. He laid the snare beneath the walnut tree and the entire flock of parrots, including the king of parrots, got their feet entangled in the mesh."

"Bastard," Bramara shuddered as he said this. Dwipada continued, ignoring the interruption.

"The king, who was a wise bird, commanded the group to flutter their wings in unison. They flew away, carrying the net and cheated the hunter of his prey and his precious net. They landed at the doorstep of a well-wisher, who freed them from their entanglement." Dwipada paused.

"You are saying then," said Vikram, "that we must act with unity?"

"No," said Dwipada. "The point of the story is that I was the well-wisher, and more importantly, the net is still with me."

"I can vouch for the strength of the net," said Bramara, "I was the parrot king of the story. That's how I came to know Dwipada."

CHAPTER TWENTY-ONE

OFF TO THEEVU

Vikram placed the feather of the *yali* with grave ceremony on a small rock and set fire to it, as his friends stood around in a circle waiting expectantly. There was no puff of smoke. No coruscating display of colors, just the stink of burnt feather. A small dot appeared on the horizon, getting bigger and bigger as it neared them.

A *yali* landed at the center of the gathering.

"Why have you summoned us?" The booming voice of the *yali* came from deep inside her head.

"Us?" Bana wondered aloud.

"*Yalis* move around in groups of four. They are in constant mental contact with each other and one speaks for all of them." Bramara explained.

"We need help," said Vikram. "Some of our friends have been abducted by a *rakshasa* and are held prisoners on an island. We need to get there to rescue them."

The *yali* looked sterner than usual.

"We don't like to meddle in the affairs of human beings. But we owe you a debt of gratitude for pointing out a nest of *nagas*, and to the human girl who helped us home in on the nest with her shout. However, I will have to consult the sisters of my quadriad before I can commit."

"You don't understand," said Vikram. "This is really urgent. Even as we speak, our friends are in great danger."

"Wait human, don't disturb our communication," said the *yali* with closed eyes.

Vikram got out of the way quickly as the *yali's* tail kept flicking for a while.

At last, the *yali* opened her eyes.

"Human, we have decided to help you."

"That's great, what I want you—"

"Wait, there are conditions," said the *yali*. "We will help you reach the place where the prisoners are kept. We will also help you in getting back but we will not fight your battles for you, unless we are attacked or if the enemy has war elephants. Do they have war elephants?" A gleam came into the *yali's* eyes. Spittle appeared at the corners of her beak.

"Not that I know of," said Vikram.

"We fight and kill only for food or in revenge. Remember, once this is over, our debt to you is repaid."

"Agreed," said Vikram, putting out the fire with his foot.

Bramara briefed the *yali*; he imprinted the directions to Theevu in her mind. It was decided earlier that Bramara would leave ahead of the others to alert Jabala and apprise her of her role in the rescue mission.

"We shall arrive at midnight," said the *yali* as she departed.

Vikram sat on a boulder looking at his forearm. He was fascinated by the way the halo on his tattoo wriggled when he made a fist. He heard a familiar whirr of wings and felt a weight on his shoulders. He continued looking at his forearm.

"You know, she actually loves you," said Bramara.

"If she does, she is doing a great job of hiding it," Vikram burst out. His tone then became guarded. "Who are you talking about?"

"Grin, grin," said Bramara and continued. "She said she loves the way your hair falls on your forehead."

"She really said that, did she?"

"No, she didn't. I am making all this up because I have nothing better to do. Come on, wake up Vikram."

Vikram looked away from his forearm and as he turned, he nearly knocked Bramara off his perch.

"If you've had as much experience as I have with women, you'll know that women have some strange ways of showing their love. Take it from me, Vik, this is just one way of showing it."

"I surely hope so. I just realized that I am fond of her."

"Just fond of her?"

"I can't think of all that now. I can think only of Aditya, who has always leaned on me for support. Besides, how can I look at anyone else before I find out who I am?"

Bramara looked at him steadily.

"Fine, I love her." He looked again at Bramara and shook his head. "I must be the only one on earth who has a parrot as a confidant."

"You will be surprised," said Bramara, "throughout history, birds have played an important role in human love affairs. Haven't you heard of go-between swans?"

The *yalis* looked menacing in the light of the flickering torches. The improvised ropes that formed a sling around the *yalis* added strange silhouettes to their already weird forms. Rope ladders made out of coconut fiber lay on the ground. Bows, arrows, javelins and swords were bundled together, ready to be loaded.

Earlier, Ponni had asked Dwipada, "Where did you get these weapons?" Dwipada cleared his throat to begin his rather long reply, "I will tell you a story." Hastily, Ponni had told him that she wanted to see if Vikram was ready, and the story remained untold.

It was decided that Vikram, Kalla, Asadu, Bana and Ponni would go with the *yalis*. Finally, everything was packed and loaded on to the beasts.

"What is this?" asked Ponni, already astride a *yali*, as she opened a small package. The package contained white flowers strung together. She couldn't stop herself from wearing them on her hair.

"Do they look all right?" She asked Vikram who was sitting just ahead of her.

Vikram could only stare in admiration.

"Your hair is a mess," said Ponni as she adjusted the flowers in her hair. "It's falling all over your forehead. Don't you use a comb?"

Vikram, who had taken all of thirty minutes with a comb to achieve an artistic effect, could only stare again.

"Oh, what a great omen! Those are *vagai* flowers, meant to be worn when you are victorious." Dwipada could only be heard faintly. The sage paused and reflected. *Seeing four* **yalis** *together is supposed to be a bad bird-omen. Oh well, I guess they cancel each other out.*

"May you return victorious!" Dwipada shouted out his blessings as the *yalis* took to the air.

CHAPTER TWENTY-TWO

THE INVASION

Cool turbulent wind blew across Vikram's face. He was acutely conscious of Ponni behind him. *Did their bodies touch or was it a trick of the wind?*

He did not know how long they had been flying. He woke up and found Ponni's arm on his shoulder. He did not move. In a short while, he felt Ponni's head on his other shoulder.

"Isn't this a lovely night, Ponni?" he said, pointing out to a bright star almost directly overhead. "That is Arundhati. It is said to have a companion star Vasishta but you can't see it. They are said to rotate about their common center of mass."

There was no reply from Ponni. He looked behind, taking care not to disturb her. Her raven-black hair had come unbound and fallen in cascades over her face. She was fast asleep.

It was still dark when Vikram sighted the island. The pentagonal outline of the island stood out clearly, and as they reached closer, the fort became more distinct. The *yalis* swung around to the south side of the island. The fort walls abutting the edge of the island came into view, albeit dimly. The *yalis* flew high, using the available cloud cover to escape detection and glide down silently, landing inside the fort walls. Vikram's *yali* was the first to land. Vikram, Kalla and Bana unloaded all the weapons and rope ladders they carried. The *yalis* vaulted over the walls and after depositing their loads, disappeared into the darkness, as silently as they came.

Almost as soon as they landed, Bramara greeted them with a low-pitched welcoming squawk, flying from shoulder to shoulder and chattering with obvious excitement.

"We go straight to Jabala's quarters but before that, we will have to get into the fort itself. They have two guards at the entrance to the fort. Normally there are many more but Jabala has ensured that there won't be too many guards on sentry duty."

They had landed very close to a guard tower in the umbra cast by the lights above.

"It will be virtually impossible to get to the fort without the guards in the tower spotting us," said Vikram.

"I can get them to come down," said Kalla, "Watch."

They watched in amazement as Kalla began climbing up the sheer walls of the tower that did not seem to have any visible handholds.

He soon came down the same way, jumping off when he was about ten feet from the ground. He displayed two daggers.

"There are two guards," he whispered. "They will soon be coming down looking for these."

Asadu and Kalla positioned themselves on either side of the entrance to the tower. Vikram stood right in front of the entrance, about ten feet away, holding an unsheathed sword in his hand. Soon enough, footsteps sounded. The guards could see Vikram clearly in the light from the tower. They charged, holding their swords aloft. They did not get much farther than Kalla and Asadu. Kalla jumped up and drop-kicked one of them, aiming for the back of the neck and felling him. The guard tried to get up when Bana rushed from his hiding place and sat heavily on him, sending him to dreamland. Asadu punched the other guard and his body hit the ground. A sound like a ton of granite hitting a metallic plate disturbed the silence of pre-dawn.

"There are some advantages to having been a stone," whispered Asadu, grinning. They kept to the shadows and reached the entrance to the main building without being detected.

The guards at the entrance were half-asleep. They awoke with a start at an insistent tapping from inside. They turned around to investigate.

They now had their backs to Bana and Asadu.

They slid down, their faces scraping the front door as they fell. Kalla made a quick search of the soldiers and found a bunch of keys. He opened the door.

Jabala and Madavi were waiting behind the door. Bramara had already alerted them.

Jabala caught Ponni in a big hug and soon they were excitedly whispering to each other.

"Come, Kalla, let's sort out the weapons," Bana called out. There was no response. He found Kalla staring at Madavi. It was easy to imagine that Kalla had his tongue hanging out. Vikram started to nudge Kalla when Madavi casually took Kalla's hand and moved away.

Vikram, along with Bana, busied himself with sorting out the weapons. They then carried everything to Jabala's room. Once or twice, he caught Jabala giving him a long and appraising look that made him turn away from her.

Vikram looked out a window. At a distance, a large contingent of soldiers was moving away from the fort and going into the flower garden on the western side of the island.

"I wonder why they are all moving away from the fort." Vikram did not realize that he had spoken aloud until Bramara answered.

"They must be busy gathering flowers. Part of Jabala's plan."

The invaders heaped all the weapons in Jabala's room and had a quick meeting. Vikram quickly recapped the plan. Bana and Asadu were in charge of distributing the weapons. Kalla and Madavi also stayed back to play their part.

Jabala led Ponni, Vikram and Bramara down a winding ramp that led to a large teakwood door with iron rings set in it.

"Just wait here," Jabala whispered to her companions before entering Trisiras's den.

CHAPTER TWENTY-THREE

AT TRISIRAS' DEN

Trisiras was lying on a couch. Beads of sweat had formed on his uncovered chest. A thick, six-foot long iron club with one end covered in sharp spikes, was propped up against the couch. Just in front of Jabala's portrait on the wall lay a huge mound of flowers in various states of decay. It almost completely obscured her picture. As Jabala entered the den, he jumped up from the couch, heads flopping around in barely suppressed excitement.

"You/Have/Come," said the middle, left and right heads simultaneously.

"Yes, I am here. My Gauri vow is complete," said Jabala, injecting enthusiasm into her voice.

"Oh, joy," said Trisiras, adjusting his voices, "and joyful celebrations. This means that I will be able to kiss you and—"

"Naughty, naughty!" Jabala interrupted him hastily. "Is this the way you behave toward all women? Tris, my piece-of-sugarcane-dipped-in-honey, you will have to wait a bit. Just do what I say."

"I have already done whatever you have asked me to do, my love. You should be really proud of me as I have done exactly as asked. Anything for you, my source of happiness, I will be delighted to do more."

"Turn around, close your eyes and count to a thousand while I go into your private grove and change into something comfortable."

"Backwards from thousand to one," she thought a bit and added. "even numbers first and then the odd ones. No cheating. Only one number at a time. Aloud. And no using your fingers to count."

"I love these games, I do," said Trisiras as he turned away from her and started counting aloud.

"One thousand," he said.

"Open Sesame," said Jabala. The doorway to the grove opened.

"Nine hundred and ninety eight." He hesitated a bit and shouted out, "What's before 998?"

"Figure it out, sweet semolina, turn around properly and no peeking," said Jabala as she gestured Vikram, Bramara and Ponni to follow her into the grove.

The grove was thick with trees of all descriptions.

"This is going to take forever," said Jabala. There was despondency in her voice.

"Not necessarily," said Vikram. From the map, we know that the grove is triangular. There are three of us, not counting Bramara. We can each start at a different apex of the triangle, move along the sides and work our way inwards. We will also keep a lookout for the pond. When you find the *peepul* tree marked with a red trident, you just have to sound a low whistle to let everyone else know that you have found it. My approximate calculations indicate that it would take no more than nineteen minutes to find the tree."

"That's not a bad idea," said Jabala. There was admiration in her voice. "In fact, we can continue our search inwards and stop at that tree." She pointed to a tree some distance away, of which only the top was visible. The tree was much taller than the rest.

Ponni perked up. "That seems like a good candidate," she said as she ran towards it, zig-zagging her way around the trees in her path.

"Wait, Ponni. Let's do it methodically," cried out Vikram.

By then, Ponni was too far away to pay heed.

Vikram and Jabala stood looking at each other in silence. Soon, Vikram heard a high pitched sound.

"Do you think Ponni is in trouble?" There was anxiety in Vikram's voice.

"No. That's her screeching out an imitation of a whistle. She never could whistle." Vikram and Jabala looked at each other for a moment and then rushed toward the sound.

The tree Ponni found was right in the middle of the garden. Its trunk was thick with age at the base and narrow toward the top. It was profusely covered with broad green leaves with elongated tips.

"You can stop screeching now," said Jabala.

"You mean, stop my whistling? Do you think that's a trident?" asked Ponni, pointing to the base of the tree. The bark of the tree had been stripped in parts.

"It does look like a trident, if you look at it so." Vikram held his head parallel to the ground and squinted to look at the tree.

"In any case, this seems to be the tallest tree in the garden. Why don't you go up the tree and see if you can locate a pond in the garden?" Jabala's request sounded like a command.

Vikram looked apprehensively at the tree.

"Be careful, Vikram. The tree seems dangerously narrow at the top."

Vikram's heart sang and he was up the tree in no time. There were many branches that grew fairly low on the trunk. Vikram had no difficulty in climbing up. He soon reached the top and looked around. There was no sign of a pond.

"No pond!" shouted Vikram.

"I thought as much," said Bramara.

"Hey, how come you didn't fly up and take a look around?" asked Vikram.

"Parrots can't see very far. Otherwise..."

Jabala had a thought. "Wait, Bramara. There is something you could do. Madavi found a lily pond from which we gathered frogs. That is possibly the only pond on the island."

"I guess I'd better find Madavi and do my messenger bit again."
Bramara launched into the air.

When Madavi and Kalla walked in, Asadu and Bana were hard at work dipping the arrowheads into a pasty substance that Madavi had provided.

"Wow," said Bana, gesticulating with an arrow that he had just finished coating, "Imagine. One scratch. You fall down. Your eyeballs start rolling. Spittle drips down the corners of your mouth. Hopefully, there will be some interesting convulsive jerking. I wonder if you will have time to say a few last words."

Asadu looked at Bana nervously and moved away a little.

"That was fantastic," said Madavi, "but you need to have the right kind of makeup on for saying such things."

"You are right," said Bana. It's virtually impossible to go on stage and sound genuine without the right kind of makeup."

"Here is the right thing for you," said Madavi as she painted Bana's face in stripes of black and red.

"How does it look?" she asked as she stepped back to admire her work.

"Scary," said Asadu. "But where have you been? What have you been up to?"

Madavi smiled. Kalla blushed. He went over to where the packages had been unloaded and busied himself.

Kalla and Madavi unpacked the rope ladders and carried them to the fort walls. Kalla threw one over the wall and shimmied up the ladder with ease. He moved up along the wall and as Madavi threw the other ladders to him, he caught them and fixed them atop the wall at six different places, one half of each hanging on either side of the wall. He stood admiring his handiwork. Through the corner of his eyes he saw an expanding multi-hued speck that quickly resolved itself into an agitated Bramara.

The parrot appeared worn out and his voice was pitched an octave higher than normal.

"Madavi! Kalla! We have work to do. There is no pond inside the grove. Jabala thinks the pond with the frogs is the one with the key in it. We have to get there to find the key to the box inside a golden lotus."

"Fine. Bana and Asadu, make sure that all the women are ready. Don't forget to look out for the signal." Kalla scowled a little as this represented a small change in the plan.

Madavi climbed up the ladder, with Kalla quite unnecessarily holding the top of the ladder. Kalla climbed down the other side quickly and Madavi followed. They dropped down to the ground and ran with Madavi leading. Bramara rode on Kalla's shoulder. They ran without making any attempt to hide as they did not meet any soldiers on their way. *Jabala's ruse has really worked.*

Eventually, they reached the pond. A frog on a lily pad looked at them impassively. The water was turbid. Kalla couldn't see the bottom.

Kalla took his shirt off and jumped into the water.

"WAIT! THOSE FROGS ARE POISONOUS!" shouted Madavi even as she realized that it was too late.

CHAPTER TWENTY-FOUR

THE MISSING KEY

Vikram too was having problems at the grove.

"We can't do much until Bramara returns. As long as you are up there, you might as well look for the box," said Jabala. Vikram looked around. The foliage was rather thick, making it difficult for him to see anything in between. He shook the branches hoping to dislodge the box. A number of yellowing leaves fell. He shifted his position on to the crook of a branch and took his gaze higher. That was when he saw it.

At first, it was a glint that caught his eye. He then looked closely. The box was nestled amidst some of the upper branches. He tried to reach the branch. The farther he climbed, the thinner were the branches. He inched higher and higher till the box was within his reach. He was about to grab the box when he heard it—a hooded cobra was poised to strike, hissing and spitting.

A chilling shock wave hit Kalla as he clove through the surface. He thought he heard Madavi shout out something, but couldn't be sure. *Thank god, the pond is reasonably deep.* Once underwater, his eyes started to burn. The water was murky. He couldn't see anything. He soon reached the bottom and started feeling around. The bottom had a thick deposit of mud and slime. His efforts only succeeded in raking up more of the mud, making the water even more opaque. His skin felt as if it were on fire. He had been holding his breath for a while now. He thought his lungs were about to rupture. He could no longer hold his breath. With a final burst of effort, he attempted to knife upwards. His foot went deeper into the mud and snagged on something.

At least it will be quick, he thought. *It shouldn't take too long for my short life to flash by in front of my eyes.* The last thing he remembered was the terrible, terrible burning...

The cobra stared at Vikram without blinking. Vikram's hands were suddenly clammy. His pulse raced. His hands gripped the branches tighter. Something clicked in his mind. Vikram did not remember where he had learned it; the mantra came to him of its own volition.

Begone, O many-splendored one, may you flourish,
Remember the words of Astika,
After the great sacrifice of Janamejaya.

He realized he had said it out aloud. The snake was no longer there. He had to rub his eyes to make sure; instead of the snake, knotted to the branch was a frayed rope, gently swaying in the breeze.

He reached for the box with trembling hands and grasped it. Ponni was right underneath the tree.

"Ponni," he called out, "I can't climb down lugging this. Catch the box."

Even as Ponni cried out, "No," he dropped the box. Ponni fumbled a little but finally caught it cleanly.

"You shouldn't have done that," said Jabala. "Trisiras may feel the jolt."

Trisiras had indeed felt the jolt. The shock rippled through his body. He snapped out of his counting like a taut bowstring that had been cut. "JABALA!" He roared.

He snatched the huge iron club resting against his couch and rushed through the passage to the grove, scattering a hillock of flowers that lay in his path.

"Okay, you may open your eyes. I know you are awake. I let you rest your head on my lap for a whole three minutes now."

Kalla opened his eyes and blinked a few times. He was about to ask 'where am I?' but changed his mind quickly when he saw Madavi's expression.

"What...happened?" he asked more feebly than he felt.

"You were very lucky. The frog's poison could have killed you, even if you had escaped drowning. Luckily, I had scrubbed and washed them all just the day before."

"There was another thing that might have saved me. As a part of my guild training, we take in small diluted quantities of different kinds of venom every day to build immunity. I'm feeling fine now. Where is Bramara and—"

"Don't talk now. Let me explain. You didn't come up for air for a long time. We had almost given you up for lost when you surfaced unconscious. Between your toes was the golden lotus with closed petals. I jumped in and dragged you to dry ground. Unfortunately, none of this was useful. Bramara searched for the key inside the lotus. There wasn't one."

Madavi's tone was listless. Her expression said it all.

They heard the roar of Trisiras awakened. Vikram's pulse quickened. Ponni checked to make sure her quiver held enough arrows. Jabala kept looking up anxiously. They had been trying to open the box. Apart from a circular depression with a number of tiny protrusions, the box appeared featureless. They could not see a separate lid. It soon became clear that there was no way to open the box without the key. However, there was no sign of Bramara.

Soon, Trisiras appeared, scything trees out of his way with his iron mace. He saw them and shouted—

"Jabala! You, you...thieving headless handmaiden of the gods." Jabala blanched at this deadly insult.

"I see that you haven't managed to open the box. Jabala, you are the worst kind of traitor. You thought you could addle my brains."

"One more reference to his three heads and I will puke," said Ponni in an aside.

"I should have learned my lesson when that sinful seductress Tilottama...anyway, that is not relevant. I am going to smash you to bits, mix it all up and eat you."

As he spoke, he got bigger. This was not because he was getting closer—he actually grew larger with every step forward.

CHAPTER TWENTY-FIVE
LIFE ESSENCE

Kalla's mind was still reeling under the effects of the poison. However, he refused to step into the depression the others seemed to be sinking into. *Is there another pond? Some other water body? Is there something we are missing?* Kalla was certain that they had missed something obvious. He decided to peer into the pond again for inspiration. Just then, Kalla's eyes caught a movement. He saw Bramara hop down from an ornate wooden pillar. The pillar had once been a support for a trellised arch, parts of which had fallen in. *Here is a dejected parrot,* Kalla thought. His eye returned again to the pillar. A carved elephant formed its base. He remembered an old couplet that Bana often recited.

The wood obscures the great mad elephant;
The mad elephant obscures the wood.

Something stirred in his mind.

"The stem, the stem," he cried. "Don't you understand? The lotus itself is the key. Remove the petals. The stem together with the seed pod is the key."

Madavi picked up the lotus they had thrown aside. The stem ended in a metallic seed pod that had a series of protuberances and depressions.

Kalla very nearly lost consciousness again as Madavi kissed him.

"Good thinking, my boy," said Bramara. "Just the sort of deduction I was about to make." He picked up the disk in his beak and was off.

Bramara was uncomfortable as he flew back to the grove. His stomach rumbled. He realized he had unconsciously eaten some of the lotus petals. He was flying rather erratically when he heard the roar. He knew something was definitely wrong. His wings beat faster. He saw the grove and Trisiras looming beside a fallen tree.

Trisiras held the club in both hands, raised high above his head. As he swung the club, Ponni drew her bow in a fluid movement, her hands a blur as three arrows sped towards the target. Trisiras halted in midstride as they hit the middle of his forehead.

Trisiras reached out and snapped off the arrows, leaving the tips in his head. For a moment, he looked at Ponni and deliberately turned his eyes away as though she was of no consequence. Jabala threw her knife with an underhand flick of her wrist. He swatted it away in mid flight with a swipe of his arm. His eyes bored into Jabala's.

"So the hand that holds flowers can hold edged weapons equally well, I see."

"Trisiras," said Jabala almost gently, "at the core, you are a strong man with a compassionate heart. Why don't you leave Pisacha?"

"Leave Pisacha? Never! Leave someone who has helped me? I am not like you, Jabala."

One set of eyes focused on the box that Vikram was holding. He saw that the box was still closed.

"Ha/Ho/He. Puny humans. You couldn't open it. Now I have all the time in the world to finish you off. And who is this chit of a girl who tries to poke me with her puny pins?"

"That's my daughter, Trisiras," Jabala said. "I hope Bramara reaches here quickly with the key," she whispered to Vikram.

"I heard that," said Trisiras. "So some friend of yours has gone looking for the key. You are waiting for him. Let him come. I only hope he is edible."

Vikram's gaze suddenly shifted to a point above and away from Trisiras' face.

"The oldest trick in the world. You think I can be diverted so easily, but look," Trisiras said. One of the heads turned around while the others continued looking at Vikram and Jabala.

It was Bramara in a screaming dive aimed at the box at Vikram's feet.

Something detached itself from Bramara and started to fall.

"THE KEY," shouted Trisiras. He let go of his club. The knotted muscles in his calves bunched up. He twisted his body around and launched into the air in a mighty leap to intercept the falling object.

"SPLAT," it landed on Trisiras's faces.

The queasiness in Bramara's stomach disappeared as he continued to dive.

It took very little time for Vikram to take the disc from Bramara and fit it in the depression on the lid of the box. The stem fitted perfectly.

Trisiras was a little dazed from the fall. He shook his heads as he stood upright and bellowed. He reached for the mace he had dropped, raised it with both hands and brought it down, aiming for Vikram's head.

Vikram's face showed determination. His right fist was clenched. The bee from the box was inside his fist. "This is for Dwipada," he said as he squeezed it, and swung away from the descending club.

Trisiras trembled like one stricken with ague. The club slipped from his hands. He cried out in a howl of pure agony.

Vikram squeezed again.

Trisiras fell down lifeless, breaking branches on his way down.

Jabala blew three short blasts on her whistle.

Madavi and Kalla heard the whistle blasts as they were walking toward the wall. They quickened their step, not making an effort to conceal themselves.

The guards who were busy gathering flowers in the garden too heard the blasts and they came out to see if they could find the source of the noise. One of them saw Madavi and Kalla. He shouted out to the others.

Soon, a detachment of a dozen guards armed with swords was running towards them. Madavi raised her arms in a gesture of surrender. Kalla followed suit. The women heard the signal and as arranged earlier, they rushed out through the rear entrance to the fort. Some of them had bows and quivers slung over their shoulders; others carried long curved swords. They rushed to the rope ladders and clambered to the top of the wall, assisted by Asadu and Bana.

Vikram knew that they had to move fast. They ran back to Trisiras's den.

"I am not sure where the other entrance is," said Jabala.

"Don't worry, we can figure it out," said Vikram. Standing in the middle of the room, he shouted 'OPEN SESAME.' They saw the wall on the other side slide back to reveal another tunnel.

"This must be the tunnel that leads from below the walls to the *rakshasa's* food store," said Jabala.

The tunnel was lit with torches. It ended in a large hall. Goat carcasses hung everywhere. The stink was overpowering.

When they emerged out of the warehouse, they saw Madavi and Kalla at a distance with their hands upraised. They also saw a group of guards advancing slowly toward the pair. The guards saw them and realizing that there were only three of them, increased their pace.

That was when a screaming horde of women descended from the rope ladders. Some of them had already reached the ground and were rushing towards them, their weapons held aloft.

They panicked at the sight of a large savage at the head of the mob, face painted hideously in black and red. The ululation scared the guards even more than the sight of the mob. Most of the guards stopped. A few who were brave enough to advance fell to poisoned arrows.

The remaining turned back and ran.

The *yalis* too had heard the preplanned signal. They took the net in their beaks. Two of them clung to edge of the steep slope, keeping the spread net flush with it, while the other two hovered with the net held taut.

Jabala directed the group. One by one, they jumped off the edge of the promontory into the waiting net below. Vikram, Ponni and Jabala had managed to clamber on to the backs of the *yalis*.

"Now I know how a bunch of fish feels when caught in a net," Kalla said. He didn't complain too much as he found Madavi on top of him.

"I feel really close to you," said Kalla.

"I need to speak to you," said Madavi.

There are worse things than the words 'I need to speak to you' in the universe but all of them have sharp teeth and long fangs. Kalla sat shaking in dreadful anticipation.

"You are smart and talented..." started Madavi.

"But," said Kalla.

"There is no 'but' in it. You should learn to take a compliment with grace."

"Yes," said Kalla, guardedly.

"I believe you can do whatever you want to do."

"What I want to do now..." Kalla's hands reached for Madavi. She pushed his hands away.

"Kalla, be serious for a moment and listen to me. With your abilities, you should be doing something else." She hesitated before proceeding.

"I know you don't want to be known as the wife of a thief, right?"

"Not exactly. I was thinking of how our sons and daughters will feel."

"Sons...daughters...? Hey, how many of them are you thinking of?"

"Don't change the topic, Kalla."

"I don't blame you. I am not happy either. But I have no choice. I don't know of any other occupation that fits me."

"You have skills. I am sure they can be used in other jobs."

127

"If only..." sighed Kalla.

"If only what?"

"Our guild has a special fund. If someone performs a truly exceptional deed, he is given a generous honorarium for life."

"I don't think you should be thinking about retirement when you have just begun work. Isn't there anything you could do?"

"Maybe, I could start a business or something."

"I think that's a great idea," said Madavi. "You have just the necessary skills for it."

CHAPTER TWENTY-SIX

BACK AT ASHRAM

The flight back to the *ashram* was uneventful, except for when one of the *yalis* thought it had seen a herd of elephants and swooped down. Thankfully, the passengers survived. Dwipada and Kamadenu were there to welcome them with garlands and bedecked the returning party with *vagai* flowers.

There was feasting and merry-making that evening. There was a huge bonfire at the *ashram*. Jabala sang. The song was melodious; the only problem was that she paused a little too often. Asadu was on the drums. Madavi and Kalla whirled to the music. Bramara tried to teach Ponni new dance steps.

Vikram stood alone under a *kadamba* tree looking at the sky. Without a hint of a cloud, the Great-Sword-in-the-Sky looked brighter than usual. The moon was clearly bidding to become full in a couple of days. A gentle breeze blew, bringing the scent of jasmine and pine. Murmuring of leaves in the forest combined with the crackling of fire set up a soothing background.

"Contemplating infinity, son?" The question woke Vikram from his reverie.

"No, *Guru* Dwipada...not really."

"Why aren't you dancing now? I just finished dancing with Ponni. You know I have a distinct advantage when I dance."

"I know, however badly you dance, you never step on your partner's toes."

"So, why aren't you dancing?"

"I just feel that there is so much more to be done. What we have achieved hasn't even scratched the surface."

"I know the feeling. Tell me something. How do you eat a rhinoceros?"

Vikram was confused.

"Er...carefully? Watching out for horns and the like. Maybe with salt and pepper?"

"Same way as you would eat an elephant. One bite at a time." Dwipada paused to allow his words to sink in before continuing.

"You have already rescued the women. This has struck a blow to Pisacha. Soon, we will administer another death blow, this time in his own backyard."

"Can this happen? Can we overcome Pisacha and ensure that Aditya and others are cured of blindness?"

"It will depend on the sincerity of your purpose."

"I am sorry, but I still don't understand how defeating Pisacha will solve our problems."

"For one thing, Pisacha will not part with Chintamani as long as he is alive. If we steal it from him, he will surely take revenge. I think I made a mistake last time in allowing him to escape. He has only become worse and he has sacrificed countless people at the altar of his deity Rakta Katteri."

"Thanks, I understand, *apeechiko*. I feel better already. I promise you that I will somehow get the Chintamani back and free Orum from its isolation." *I will ensure that no more children in Orum become blind.*

"Now go and dance. Someone seems to be looking for you."

Even from a distance, Vikram sensed Ponni's eyes were on him.

Vikram busied himself helping the women pack their belongings. They were anxious to return home. Carrier pigeons had already been sent to the people of Akkam and Bakkam, informing them of the rescue of the women.

A couple of women bid Vikram a fond farewell by caressing his cheeks and cracking their knuckles to ward off evil eye. Vikram was happy to see them finally astride on mules. The task of escorting them back to Akkam and Bakkam fell to Asadu who was strutting around. Jabala, Ponni and Madavi opted to stay back. Asadu had arranged for several mules to transport the women. For himself, he found a black horse with a white star on its forehead.

From a distance, Dwipada was berating Asadu.

"Why do you have to hire an expensive horse with a star on its forehead?"

"I know sir, you were about to say, 'money does not grow on trees'. I painted the white star." Seeing Dwipada's expression, he added, "It makes me look dashing, sir."

"No more cheek from you. Be off with you!"

CHAPTER TWENTY-SEVEN
ABHISHTU AND DUBAKU

Dubaku was not a boat. He was also not lying down. If he were one and so positioned, you could say that he was broad in the beam. In fact, he was thick in bow and stern as well.

Dubaku and Abhishtu were like chalk and cheese. They were more like a limestone hillock and a dinky cheese that had been badly sliced and left on a dirty kitchen countertop for a long time. Dubaku looked intently at his uncle Abhishtu with cow eyes, as he walked alongside him.

"Uncle, this is great. Mandala is so much bigger than my village."

"Pisacha's bathroom is bigger than your village. Just look around and listen carefully to me."

"Yes I will, uncle! My mother sent me to you to learn. She said, "You listen carefully to that bas—"

"I know. My sister can be rather forceful. You should never repeat what people say."

"Never repeat what people say," said Dubaku.

Abhishtu groaned. He looked disparagingly at Dubaku. This failed to have any impact on his nephew, as the direction of his look changed by some sixty degrees or so because of his squint.

"Let me explain something about this city. Mandala has eight levels of defenses against intrusion into the citadel. Each of the eight concentric walls surrounding the city has only one entrance. Each level poses a unique challenge to anyone who wishes to enter the city. No one has been known to get past more than two of these walls."

"What is concentric, uncle?"

"A very good question. You are certainly a guard material. You can be one of the guards at the logical gates. I think you will make an excellent knave."

"What are the other types, uncle?"

"There are knights, but that's—"

"What do knaves and knights get to wear uncle?" When Dubaku sank his claws into something, he stuck to it with the tenacity of an *udumbu*.

"Knaves normally wear black leather and knights wear shiny armor. But that is not important."

"I will be only a knight, uncle. I will wear shiny armor. If you don't get me the job, I will tell *amma*."

"On second thought, knaves also wear shiny armor, just to fool people into thinking they are knights."

Dubaku turned his nose up at being a knave. He stopped in the middle of the road and stood with his arms akimbo. He pouted and said, "I want to be a knight."

"Fine, you can be one. Just write to your mother and tell her your uncle is looking after you extremely well."

"But I can't write, uncle."

"Uncle..." Abhishtu's squint deepened. "Now, what?"

"I forgot, uncle, it is so difficult to think and talk at the same time... ah yes, now I remember. Do you have the power to make me a guard, uncle?"

"Of course." Abhishtu preened a little. "I am the most important official—the prime minister of Pisacha's kingdom. Now, do you have any more questions?"

"Yes. What happens if someone gets through all the gates, uncle?"

"Ha ha, if someone, as you say, gets through the gates, he is given the greatest honor."

"I know what that means. He is garlanded, welcomed, wedded to the kingdom and given half the king's daughter. That seems ridiculous. Depends how the cut is made, I guess. Either way, there are problems."

"Just stop! And stop thinking. My sister often talks about the headaches you get after this kind of binge thinking. True, the one who gets through all the gates will be garlanded. He will have a fate no worse than marriage—he will be sacrificed to goddess Rakta Katteri. Anyway, now I have to be on board the *Kollivai*. I have no more time to waste with you."

CHAPTER TWENTY-EIGHT

NECROMANCY

"By tomorrow," Pisacha said, "the moon will be full. Sometime after midnight, it will be consumed by the serpent Ketu..."

"So will the virgins, boss," added Abhishtu.

"Rubbish, how is Ketu going to eat up the virgins?" Pisacha snapped at him.

"I only meant to say..." Abhishtu stopped, realizing that his master was not interested.

They were on the upper deck of the ship *Kollivai*, which was now rapidly approaching Theevu.

"Rakta Katteri will be pleased," said Pisacha.

As he stared at the familiar outlines of Theevu, Abhishtu could sense that something was wrong. Pisacha was staring intently at a group of soldiers who were rushing towards the ship instead of waiting for inspection in orderly lines at the shore.

Pisacha and Abhishtu were first to reach the shore after they dropped anchor.

"What's wrong?" asked Pisacha, his face tight with anger.

"Er...everything," said the commander of the fort in a squeaky voice, which shook uncontrollably in unison with his heavy body. "All the women have escaped. Some people invaded the island and freed them."

Thunder and lightning danced on Pisacha's face.

"What do you mean by 'took'? Who were they? How did they get away? What was Trisiras doing? More importantly, WHAT WERE YOU ALL DOING?"

The commander's silhouette blurred a little as he shook even more.

"Trisiras is dead, sir. And we were busy gathering flowers, sir." For a moment, Pisacha could not find the right words to utter.

"DEAD? And you were picking FLOWERS?" Pisacha thundered.

The commander perhaps judged this to be a rhetorical question and simply hung his head.

"That was not a rhetorical question," said Pisacha. "I would like to know why you were engaged in the oh-so-important job of picking flowers rather than being on guard duty."

"Trisiras desired it, sir. He had to quadruple the flowers every day, sir. On the day in question, we were ordered to gather four thousand ninety six flowers, sir."

"There aren't four thousand flowers on the island," said Abhishtu.

"No, sir."

"Then how did you gather that many?" asked Abhishtu.

"We didn't, sir. We kept searching."

"Nobody saw them get away?"

"We did, sir. But they were howling like hungry wolves, waving about swords and clubs before they charged us, sir. They also shot poisoned arrows at us. The soldiers nearest to them were killed, sir."

"Still, you do not have the slightest idea who helped them escape."

The commander hung his head. The peacock feather on his helmet drooped a little.

Pisacha appeared calm. Almost gently, he said, "I am tickled to death. So must you be." He nodded to Abhishtu and said, "See to it."

The commander grinned evilly.

"Yes, sir," said Abhishtu, "apparently they have some of the finest Ganda Beranda feathers. We will—"

"Just see to it," snapped Pisacha.

The commander was led away.

"Who is this woman?" he asked, looking at Trijada, who stood silently with her hands folded, looking down meekly.

"That is Trijada," said the newly appointed commander.

"She looked after Trisiras. She made sure he had enough to drink and cleaned his room of the after effects."

"If he had enough to drink," said Pisacha, "his room would need to be cleaned anyway."

Abhishtu looked at what he thought was in Pisacha's direction.

"Ha, ha," added Pisacha.

"Ha, ha," said Abhishtu in a monotone.

"I don't like the way you laugh," said Pisacha. "You need training."

He then turned to Trijada. "Do you know who the attackers were?"

Trijada remained mute.

"Obviously, no one knows who the attackers were, where they came from or where they went. I will find out my way. Make sure that this woman comes back with us. I like to have pale-complexioned women around me. I am also a little short of domestic help at the castle," said Pisacha.

Though Pisacha appeared composed, Abhishtu knew that he was most dangerous when he appeared calm.

"Have you already cremated the bodies?" asked Pisacha.

'No, sir, we were planning on a mass cremation this evening for Trisiras and his men," one of the men spoke up.

"Bring the bodies to the cremation ground and let me know when you are done."

The biers were made of bamboo scaffolding, tied together with coconut fiber ropes. The one on which Trisiras's body lay was much bigger than others'.

The sky was overcast. Now and then the clouds parted, revealing a gibbous moon. Somewhere a wolf howled. Or maybe not, because no one at Theevu heard it. It was the kind of night where you expect wolves and bats to be active.

Abhishtu and the newly appointed commander stood awkwardly in attention. Pisacha sat cross-legged on the body of a soldier in full uniform. He was facing Trisiras's huge carcass.

"Hey, you," said Pisacha.

Half a dozen voices said, "Yes, sire."

He pointed to one of the bodies near Trisiras'. "Put him on the bier and light it," he ordered. A dozen guards scurried.

Tongues of flame leaping from the pyre cast arabesques of light on Pisacha's face. The moon was once again obscured by the clouds and the only light available came from the pyre.

He closed his eyes and began muttering incantations under his breath. Now and again, angry plosive stops burst from his lips. He spat out the 'Vashats' and 'Phats'. At times, Pisacha's hands were entwined in complex hand gestures, moving with the confidence of a striking snake.

Trisiras's eyes flew open. Abhishtu was no longer sure that they were closed to begin with. They reflected the fire in an eerie glow. The speed of the incantation picked up. The fire spluttered and crackled. Shadows danced on Trisiras's face.

Did Trisiras' lips part a little? Did a sigh escape his lips? Abhishtu stared, fascinated.

"Why...are you...bringing me...back?" This time, it was certainly no trick of the imagination.

"I urge you to answer me." Pisacha's voice held more than a hint of command.

A long period of silence was broken by the occasional snap of embers.

"Answer me or I will feed your carcass to jackals and dogs." Pisacha hissed.

"Make it...quick. I cannot...linger. I am about to be...reborn. The foreplay has...already...begun."

"Tell me, who killed you?"

"I don't...know. It must be Jabala..."

"Who is Jabala?"

"...Or her daughter...Or that bird that shat on me... Or that impudent boy..."

"Who was that boy?"

"I...don't...know."

"There must be something he said that you remember."

"He said...he said..." The corpse's voice was fast fading. "He said... this one is for...Dwipada."

The corpse's eyes closed shut as Pisacha's hand went involuntarily to where his nose should have been and his lips curved up in a cruel smile.

Pisacha paced to and fro in apparent agitation.

"I should have guessed that Dwipada is behind all this. We set sail for Mandala immediately. As soon as we get back, I want you to send someone to Dwipada's *ashram* and gather information. I am sure this is part of Dwipada's plan to get back at me."

"A spy, sir? I could send my nephew Dubaku. He is young but he is a sincere boy."

'No. No. Not your sister's son." Pisacha shuddered as he remembered him from his interview. We will send Dussakuni."

"Yes, boss."

CHAPTER TWENTY-NINE

THE SPY

Dwipada's voice had a hypnotic quality to it.

"Keep your eyes closed. Now, be aware of sounds that are external to you. Hear the birds chirping at a distance on your left. Hear the wind whistling. Shift your focus from sound to sound without lingering, without forming an attachment."

Vikram heard the birds, the cicadas and the wind whispering through the trees.

"Now, slowly let your awareness detach itself from the external world and focus on your breath. As you inhale...hear the rustling..."

"Rustling...in my breath?" Vikram was nonplussed.

"No, no. I can hear someone in the bushes. Get up." Dwipada ran towards the direction of the sound. Vikram got up and ran behind him. They soon reached a clearing. There was no one there.

"What's this?" Vikram saw a red mark, shaped like a spearhead on the ground, glistening in the light of the full moon.

Dwipada leaned forward, back straight, scraped a bit off the red mark and applied it to the tip of his tongue.

"Hmm..." he said. "Juice of the betel leaf. A mixture of betel and quick lime." Vikram maintained a politely quizzical expression.

"The minions of Pisacha are known to chew betel leaves with quicklime. One thing is clear—we have a spy. We need Kamadenu and Madavi on this one." Vikram ran ahead to fetch Madavi and requested her to accompany them. By the time they reached Kamadenu's shed, Dwipada was already there.

"Gauri, I would like you to come with us."

Kamadenu pointedly looked away from them.

"I am sorry," said Dwipada. "Kamadenu, please come with us."

Kamadenu turned her head and looked at them.

"There is a spy somewhere in the forest. We need you to sniff him out," Vikram said.

"Do you have any of his personal effects? Anything that has his smell? Except for loincloth, I don't do loincloth."

"No, just come with us. We know where the spy has been."

They walked to the spot where they had seen the red mark.

"This is the juice of betel leaf, chewed with quick lime and betel nut shavings...wait, this is terrible." Kamadenu sounded hugely affronted as she continued.

"He has added some *gorochana*—bile stones from the gall bladder of a cow."

"Right, but can you tell us which way the spy went?" asked Vikram.

"That I intend to find out. It is personal now," said Kamadenu, her face looking grim.

She kept her nose to the ground as she followed the spoor, lifting her head once in a while to sniff the air. Soon, they reached a glade where they heard voices. Vikram warned Kamadenu to stay back and hide behind a clump of bushes. Madavi and he followed suit. As they watched, a short man in black robes spoke into a crystal, which answered him back. "Boss, I will get the information soon. I have already overheard certain conversations. I know, for instance, that they are training."

"Who is training and what were they training for? I needed the information as of yesterday."

The voice was oddly metallic. This was either distortion caused by the crystal or that was the natural voice of the speaker.

"I am talking about today, boss. There was this boy, who probably hasn't even started shaving and an incredibly old man with an ugly face. They were, I think, meditating."

"Meditating, what?"

"Meditating, *boss*."

"Dussakuni, you better have something more substantial to report. I want to know how many people there are, what their plans are, even what they had for breakfast and dinner."

"Yes, boss, I can easily find out what they had for dinner. I am trained in the arcane art of analyzing fecal matter. I can nip around to their toilets—"

"I don't care a...shut up and listen. Just let me know what their plans are. Concentrate on that ugly-faced Dwipada. Report to me exactly at this time the day after tomorrow. I will be waiting for your call."

The odd droning sound that accompanied the voice went dead.

"I am sure that was my old friend, Pisacha," said Dwipada, stepping into the clearing.

"And don't reach for your knife." Vikram emerged from the bushes with a sword in hand.

While Dussakuni was clearly startled, his next reaction was inexplicable. His eyes were fixed on something beyond Dwipada and Vikram. Fear was palpable in his eyes.

"The...that cow. Please keep it away from me."

"If you come quietly with us, she won't harm you," said Madavi.

Dussakuni was sweating profusely. "I was once gored by a cow."

"You probably deserved it," Kamadenu sounded stern. "What kind of a man chews *gorochana* with his betel leaf?"

"O gods! A talking cow. What have I done to deserve this?"

"Actually, in your previous birth—" began Dwipada.

"Just behave yourself," Vikram spoke sharply to Dussakuni. "Kamadenu is the kind of cow that can gore you to death and brag about it to cattle and humans alike."

Kamadenu raised an eyebrow.

"I will come...quietly," said Dussakuni.

"Your eyelids are heavy," said Madavi. "You are feeling sleepy."

"Not really," said Dussakuni.

"I can always call Kamadenu."

"Now that you mention it, I am sort of feeling sleepy." Dussakuni closed his eyes.

"You will wake up the moment I utter the phrase *'choo mandrakkali'*. You will answer all our questions truthfully and tell us everything you know about Pisacha Pinda."

She paused for a moment and when Dwipada nodded, said *'choo mandrakkali'*.

"Where does Pisacha live?" asked Madavi.

"Pisacha is the absolute ruler of the walled town of Mandala, which is about two days march due west from here. It is immediately after the valley of ghosts. He lives inside his castle within the town."

"How often are you expected to report back to Pisacha?"

"Every alternate day at sundown, the crystal lights up. That's when I talk to him."

"Describe the castle and its security."

"There is a large central structure connected to four other tower-like buildings. This is surrounded by eight concentric walls, which are fifteen meters high. Each wall has only one entry point. To gain entry at each point, one has to overcome an ordeal. It is rumored that no outsider has gone beyond the second wall."

"What kind of ordeals are these?"

"No one knows except for the guards and Pisacha. Abhishtu, his minister or rather his factotum, may know a little more. I have heard rumors that these tasks test physical, mental and even magical skills to the extreme."

"How many fighting men does he command?"

"Around a thousand trained fighters. In all, about five thousand people live inside the walled city."

"Why has he sent you?"

"He said 'I want to finish off that ugly-faced Dwipada. I want to destroy his *ashram* and his friends within a month'."

Dwipada, who stood behind Dussakuni, was obviously agitated. He waved his hands up and down and finally managed to attract Madavi's attention.

"Chintamani," he mouthed.

"Think of money," said Madavi.

"I always do," replied Dussakuni.

"No, no. Chintamani," said Dwipada aloud.

"Yes, I know. Chintamani."

"Where does Pisacha keep it?" Madavi asked.

"It is around the neck of Rakta Katteri's image."

"And where is this neck, I mean, image?"

"It is in an underground cave temple below the main castle. Its main entrance is in Pisacha's chambers, which he keeps locked. The other entrance is one-way."

"What do you mean by one-way?"

"You can only enter. If you try to get back out, you get killed."

"Nice. This Pisacha seems like a nice person."

"No, no. People hate him."

Madavi glanced at Dwipada. He cleared his throat and pointing to his own face said, "This face of mine is not ugly. It is beatific, peaceful and...um...beautiful."

"But it is mostly beard."

"You too have a beard."

"Yes, I have a face that is distinct from the beard. You have a beard that may or may not hide a face."

"What is seen is beautiful. You hear?"

"Yes," said Dussakuni. "I hear and I obey."

"You will forget everything that you have said, seen or heard the moment you hear the trigger word. This evening, you will report to Pisacha. Further, you will say that you have assessed the strengths of Dwipada and the others and that they are extremely weak. Also, tell him we intend to come to Mandala to reason with him. *Choo mandrakkali.*"

CHAPTER THIRTY

THE TRAINING

The sun hadn't risen yet. The western sky was drenched in a red luminescence in all its refracted glory. Vikram stood in the middle of a field with Bramara skittering around impatiently. Two bundles of straw were suspended by steel chains from a branch of a ficus tree about two hundred paces from where they stood.

"Say the invocative prayer for the Ten in your mind before beginning the practice," instructed Bramara.

Vikram remembered the passage from the Gnomon.

There are gods for everything, except maybe for teeth. They had it real easy. Since there were so many of them, some functions were carried out by more than one god. To be exact, there were three hundred and thirty million of them. For an estimated human population of thirty million, there were about eleven gods per head. To be able to achieve success, particularly for mastering the *astras*—the divine missiles—one needed to propitiate ten gods. Not any ten gods but the ones that one was assigned to.

"Done," said Vikram after reciting the prayers for each one of the gods.

"The five elemental *astras* now," shouted Bramara, "fire, *Agneyastra*."

Vikram closed his eyes for a moment, muttered the mantra, drew an arrow from the quiver on his shoulder and released it. The straw bundles burst into flames.

"Water, *Varunastra*."

Soon the flames were quenched and the bundle was soaked in a flood of water.

"Air, *Vayu.*"

A gust of wind blew at the bundle and the chain swung crazily.

"Earth, *Prithvi.*"

Even before the arrow struck the bundle, a giant hand seemed to reach out and pummel the target with such power that thick links of the chains snapped and the bundles struck the ground with great force.

"Ether, *Akasha.*"

One moment the bundle was whole and the next, the bundle and the chain disintegrated into nothingness.

"Switch hands now."

This threw Vikram off.

"The bow in your right hand and the arrow in your left."

They went through target practice again after replacing the bundles.

At last, Bramara seemed satisfied.

"You are almost ready now. You are well on the way to becoming a true *savyasachi*—the ambidextrous one."

"Are you dreaming now?" asked Bramara for the fifth time that day.

Vikram shifted his awareness to the little finger of his right hand, as he was taught, lifted it and looked at it critically.

"No."

"We will continue our dream practice tonight," said Bramara.

Ponni was hard at work under Jabala. Kamadenu and Chetak assisted her. Chetak had finished teaching her the thirty-six ways of biting and sixteen ways of kicking an opponent, with special emphasis on male opponents. Kamadenu had taught her all about head-butting.

Jabala seemed happy with the progress her daughter was making.

"I think you are ready," said Jabala.

Vikram was exhausted. He fell asleep as soon as he lay down.

He was in the midst of a desert. He was alone and his throat was parched. He heard the voice: "Be aware of your little finger."

Automatically, he took his awareness to the little finger of his right hand. He lifted it up to see. He was surprised to see the nail on the finger was now a sharp talon. He looked at his arm. The tattoo hadn't disappeared. It was, however, different. Instead of a single sword, his arm displayed a field of swords. He could see another lion—or was it a lioness—seated next to the rampant lion. He then knew he was dreaming.

"Lush green grass," he heard a voice. He turned to look at a middle-aged man with a kind face.

"What do you mean? This is a desert."

But when he turned around again, there was undulating greenery everywhere.

"Mountains," he thought or said, he wasn't sure which.

The scene around him changed. He could see lofty snow covered peaks all around. A path spiraled up the nearest mountain.

He was excited. He had never been able to control his dreams before.

"Wake up," the voice said and then even more insistently, "Wake up!"

He opened his eyes.

"Don't move now. Recall all the details of the dream and write it down in your dream journal," said Bramara.

"...I believe, therefore, that we should move in now and finish Pisacha. We should not wait for him to attack the *ashram*." Dwipada seemed to be winding up to this. All of them were gathered at the hall of sacrifice to discuss what they should do next.

"Offense is the best form of defense," said Bana. "However, deer do not willingly enter the mouths of sleeping lions..."

Bramara did not even bother to acknowledge Bana's remarks. "I think Vikram and Ponni are ready now. Also, Pisacha believes that we are weak. He will be careless. Besides, he believes that we will be defeated by his test at the eight gates. To play along is our best chance."

"We can gather an army from Akkam and Bakkam. After all, their wives, daughters and sisters were held prisoners. I am sure we will be able to get at least a couple of hundred fighters to back our cause," said Asadu.

"It is better not to be prepared at all than be underprepared," quoted Bana.

"I believe there is no point in going against Pisacha with a large army," said Dwipada. "He will surely see us coming and prepare for a war. There is no way we can raise a large enough one to match Pisacha's. It is much better for Pisacha to see it as a personal mission."

"I too think Vikram and Ponni are reasonably prepared for the confrontation to come," said Asadu.

"I am fine," said Vikram. "I think I am ready. Bramara called me a *savyasachi* the other day. Let's go," said Vikram.

"Does it mean you get to wash your behind with either hand?" whispered Bana.

Vikram hoped that Ponni had not heard the remark. He looked at her for a moment, bemused by her large sparkling eyes. She gave no indication of having heard it. He barely heard her say, 'I too am ready'.

"I know you are itching to see some action." Dwipada's tone held a warning. "However, please be warned that there will be many dangers on the way. Of course, these are nothing compared to what you will face at the castle. The worst will be if Pisacha wins when you finally confront him."

"You mean the danger of him killing us?" said Vikram.

"Worse," said Dwipada.

"What can be worse than getting killed?" asked Ponni, her face clouded in puzzlement.

Bramara spoke eventually.

"He will become the most powerful being on earth. He loves nothing more than enslaving everyone to do his bidding. Let us not dwell on that. We have to make some plans. I believe that we should start immediately. If we wait another week or so, the situation at Orum will become irreversible."

They discussed various plans of action late into the night.

CHAPTER THIRTY-ONE

OFF TO MANDALA

Asadu had arranged for eight horses. Vikram rode on Chetak. Bana had wanted a warhorse that could bite and kick an enemy into submission.

"Here you are," said Asadu, handing over the reins of a nondescript horse to Bana, "one warhorse per specifications."

"Looks like the only thing it has bitten is its own tongue."

"Yes, I know, very deceptive, isn't it? Can lull the enemy."

Asadu was on his white horse with a star on its forehead. Initially, Madavi started out sidesaddle but seeing Jabala and Ponni, she too rode her horse straddling it. Ponni was bestride Uchchisravas, a white filly with a jet-black tail. Kalla mounted a brown horse on which he had thrown a saddle of brown leather with green splotches. He claimed that it rendered him near invisible.

They carried their weapons of choice. Vikram had a sword at his side that was curved just enough to cut and thrust. This was the weapon with which he had been practicing with Asadu.

"What's your preferred weapon?" Asadu asked Bana.

"I am carrying my scriber," said Bana.

Bana showed Asadu the scriber. It was longer than usual and the tip was ground down to a needle-sharp point.

"This is actually called a sheafer as it can pierce through a sheaf of thirty palm leaves without effort." Bana explained.

"Better than a sword, eh?" asked Asadu.

"Well, could be, especially since I have treated the tip with snake venom."

Jabala and Ponni brought along sharp daggers, tipped with frog venom. Jabala's were of her own design. They had detachable tips that could be left behind in the victims' bodies. The tips had small but very sharp, backward-pointing serrations which made it virtually impossible for them to be pulled out. She carried spare tips in a pouch.

Ponni also carried a bow and a set of fletched arrows.

Dwipada carried an ax with an edge sharp enough to slice a feather.

Kalla carried a length of steel wire and a set of stout sticks. He also had a black box with assorted tools of his trade. Asadu had a set of sticks with some of them sharpened and hardened at their ends to function as spears.

"I thought we would meet all kinds of dangers while traveling through the forbidden forest. This has been a left-handed play so far." Vikram remembered the last time he had traversed the forest.

"What does that mean?" Ponni looked perplexed.

"Oh, it's just a term we use in Orum. It denotes an action that's so easy it can be done using your left hand."

"Hey, you know I am left-handed, don't you?"

"That's really cool," said Vikram.

"I know," piped in Asadu who had ridden closer. "I really pity Jabala for having a daughter who is dark-skinned and left-handed."

Asadu had the experience of being turned into a stone. But if Ponni's look had the intended effect, he would have turned to ashes.

"I wonder why we haven't had that many problems on the way," continued Vikram.

"That's simple. All the denizens of the forest have heard of my master's reputation," said Asadu. "Even the really dark beings that inhabit this place shiver and keep away on sensing my master's presence."

It was late evening when they reached the foothills of the Agastya mountain. They pressed on through a pass into a valley.

Vikram had a strange feeling as though something was crawling on the back of his neck.

"Why do you keep turning around?" asked Kalla.

"I don't know," said Vikram. "I have a feeling we are being watched."

There was a chill in the air. The sounds of birds and insects, which had formed a constant background, seemed to have stopped.

"I am tired," declared Chetak, "I cannot move another foot."

"What was that? Don't you speak Horse?" asked Uchchisravas, who was trotting along.

"I am sorry, my dear. These humans can't understand anything other than their language. You too must be tired, my poor dear," neighed Chetak.

"Don't you 'poor dear' me. If you talk down to me, I will—"

Chetak interrupted her, knowing that when horses talk about what they can do to each other, they can get pretty graphic.

"No, no. Don't get me wrong." He looked around desperately for an appropriate continuation to the conversation and found it.

"You are a pretty filly, I must say. I particularly like your black tail, which sort of sets off your color."

"I am actually white all over," said Uchchi.

"What? I can clearly see your tail. No one has ever said that my vision is blinkered. I am sure your tail is black."

"Want to bet?" challenged Uchchi.

"Of course, your tail is black. Are you blind or something?"

"Sorry," said Uchchi, "It was an obscure reference."

"Watch and learn," said Chetak, "I am tired, and I am going to complain loudly." This was also in Horse.

Chetak then stopped cold. He splayed his forelegs and let out a whinny. It looked as though he would fall down at any moment. Seeing this, Dwipada called a halt to the party.

"I really was hoping to avoid stopping here, but we don't have too many options. The horses really seem to be tired. This is the valley of ghosts. This is a dangerous place, particularly at night. The beings that inhabit this place prey on your fears and doubts. Whatever you do, don't show any signs of emotional weakness."

"We will set up camp here. As long as you follow my instructions carefully, there should be no problems." But the lines of worry could be seen or at least imagined, even through his beard.

Asadu and Bana busied themselves unloading packages. Vikram and Kalla were sent out to gather firewood. By the time they returned, three tents had been erected.

"Asadu, where are my *arani* sticks?"

"They are in the folds of your clothes, sir," said Asadu.

Dwipada inserted the upper stick into the notch on the lower one and rubbed them together vigorously till it started a roaring fire.

"Listen to me, all of you. I am going to draw a protective line around the tents. None of you will step outside the circle, no matter what. Kalla, Vikram and Bana will take turns keeping a watch. We will leave this place in the morning."

Saying this, Dwipada took one of the fire sticks, and drew a large circle on the ground encompassing all three tents, while muttering incantations. When he was finished, the circle shone with a green glow.

CHAPTER THIRTY-TWO
DUSSAKUNI AND PISACHA

Dussakuni was squatting in one of the *ashram's* toilets, when he heard a low hum. He searched in the folds of his garments and fished out the crystal. It was pulsating a vivid red. He touched a small knob on its side and held it to his ear.

"What have you got to report now?" the metallic voice sounded in his ear.

"Plenty, boss. Lots of *apupa*. Wheat cakes mixed with jaggery, boss. Some river fish too. You know, river fish have this distinctive odor and taste, especially after digestion. Also fruits..."

"I am not interested in what the people at the *ashram* ate, you idiot."

"Horse, boss?"

"They ate horses?"

"No boss. I can tell you what the horses ate."

"I don't want to know the food habits of any living thing. Just get to the point."

"But you said, boss..."

"FORGET what I said. What are they doing?"

"They have just left, boss. They aim to reason with you to give up the Chintamani and also to stop the practice of virgin sacrifice."

"Hahaha. That is the best thing I have heard from you. They want to reason with me, eh? I will be sure to carry my better self with me so they can appeal to it till their eyes start foaming. How many of them are coming? Is that evil-faced Dwipada in the group?"

"You mean the beautiful, peaceful, beatific-faced Dwipada, boss?"

"Ha, ha. That was funny. I didn't know you could be sarcastic."

"No, boss. Yes, boss, Dwipada is part of the group. I counted seven others, boss. This includes three women. I had talked about a boy earlier. I have learned that his name is Vikram. Dwipada's assistant is one among them."

"You have done well, Dussakuni. I think I will allow them to, haha, try and reason with me. Assuming, of course, that they get past the valley of ghosts and the eight gates of Mandala."

"Unless they too become ghosts." Dussakuni's face lit up with a smile.

"What will happen if they become ghosts?" asked Pisacha testily.

"They can pass through the gates, sire."

"Shut up! Don't talk nonsense! Wait, you can be of further use. Follow them for a while and gather as much information on them before you return. I am particularly interested in that boy."

"Yes, boss."

"And I may drop in on them...er...virtually."

The connection was broken.

CHAPTER THIRTY-THREE

VALLEY OF GHOSTS

Vikram was back at Orum. He could see his brother Aditya through a haze. Aditya jeered at him.

"You are not fit to be a potter. Look at me. I have my father's nose and his color. You..."

The voice and the image faded, only to be replaced by Vikram's philosophy teacher's. He was pointing to a portrait that Vikram could see clearly, except for the face. He screamed or thought he had when he saw that the face had no features. The face was blank and seemed to reflect images from around.

"This man's son is not your father's son. Who isn't he?"

The scene dissolved and his mother appeared. "I am sorry. Actually, he has features. They are inside the box. What I did was for your own good. And the country. And the gods. And all living and non-living and non-vegetarian beings. Ask Daivagan. He is vegetarian except that he eats fish. Your father is very fond of fish."

"Wake up, wake up. It's your turn now."

"No," mumbled Vikram, "I am not fond of fish. I won't eat it."

The voice became insistent. Vikram woke up. He found that he was trembling and covered in sweat. He saw Kalla bending over him.

"Do you want me to keep watch for some more time?" Kalla's voice showed concern.

"I am fine," said Vikram. "It was just a dream."

Even before Vikram could finish speaking, Kalla was lying flat on the ground. Vikram shook his head. He heard some sounds from the prone Kalla.

"What's that?" he asked. There was no reply. He realized that Kalla was mumbling in his sleep and exited the tent.

The moment he stepped out, he felt a blast of cold air. He shivered and pulled his shawl tighter around his neck. He remembered his mother Durga saying, "Cover your ears. You will catch a cold otherwise." He remembered how she followed her own advice, particularly when she was expecting Aditya. She was always wrapped up in a shawl, a muffler over her head and cotton in her ears, even in midsummer. He wondered if she did that when she was pregnant with him.

In the dim light of a fire, he could see dry leaves on the ground. Vikram realized with a shock that they weren't disturbed by the breeze.

He tried to scream—a feeble cry emanated from him before his throat seized shut. A hazy mist surrounded him. He heard voices that he vaguely recognized. The voices were beckoning him.

In a fugue, he stumbled forward. A phosphorescent glow struck his eyes. *I was warned not to cross this line.* The voices grew insistent. He could distinguish the really strident individual voices amidst the cacophony.

"Come, come to me, my son." This was his father Kuyavan's voice.

"We are really missing you. Come back. Come to me." Durga was coaxing him.

Without thinking, Vikram stepped across the line. The world started to close in on him. His head filled with screeches and screams. He fell down, his mind a maelstrom of chaotic thoughts and emotions.

Kalla looked miserable. "He is dead. It's my fault. He seemed tired. I shouldn't have allowed him to take over guard duty." He bent over Vikram's still form and tried to feel the pulse on his wrist.

"Don't touch him," shouted Dwipada.

Kalla withdrew his hand hastily.

"He is in an extremely weak state. He has been infected by several denizens of this place. The prognosis isn't good. He will get weaker and weaker and die in a couple of hours." Dwipada started pacing up and down, deep in thought.

"We can't give up like that. Tell me what I can do." Ponni's back was straight and her eyes were clear when she spoke.

"Bring me the box Vikram brought from home," spoke Bramara, who had been looking at Vikram critically all along.

Ponni went into the tent and brought out the box after a brief search.

Dwipada manipulated Vikram's hand so that it touched the top of the box, taking extreme care to see that no part of the Vikram's body touched him. The box snapped open. It now held a large gold ring with some kind of an insignia on it.

"Slip it on his ring finger. Make sure you don't touch him." Bramara screeched out the instructions. Ponni was the first to act. She snapped off a length of silk thread from her skirt, tied it to the ring and carefully worked it around Vikram's ring finger on his left hand.

As they watched, the ring turned smoky-grey first and then jet-black. On Bramara's instructions, Ponni eased off the ring and threw it away. The ring rolled away. In a few minutes, the ring disappeared in a puff of smoke. Vikram opened his eyes. With great effort, he indicated that he was thirsty. Ponni went to get him a glass of water. Dwipada felt Vikram's pulse.

"The danger is not past. It will be touch-and-go. Even if he survives, he may not be his old self again. He needs the care of a skilled physician." Dwipada said.

Jabala bent over Vikram and examined him, feeling his pulse. Then she peeled back Vikram's eyelids and examined his eyes. She then put her ears to his chest and listened.

"The only thing that could save him is the extract of Sanjeevini herb. I have it with me. If he is conscious after I give him the medicine, he will have major convulsions. That may kill him."

There was silence all around. Dwipada finally broke the silence.

"Bramara, there is no other option. You have to teach him the one thing you have been holding back," said Dwipada. "I guess so," said Bramara and flew off into the forest.

Jabala looked at Dwipada with a quizzical expression.

"You will know soon enough." Dwipada smiled.

Ponni felt a lump in her throat. She tried to blink away her tears.

A sudden rustling in the bushes caught her attention. A wild pig rushed into the clearing and halted unsteadily on its shaky legs. Ponni raised her bow in an instant and nocked an arrow.

"NO," shouted Dwipada.

Ponni lowered the bow and dropped the arrow back into her quiver. The pig fell down stiff, legs up in the air. Almost immediately, Bramara flew back from the cover of the trees.

"No pigs have been harmed in this experiment. It was dead to begin with," said Dwipada.

Seeing blank stares all around, Dwipada added, "*Koodu vittu koodu.*"

The stares were still unstained. Jabala, however, nodded intelligently.

Bramara flew in and perched on Jabala's shoulders. "If you administer the medicine, how long will it take for the reaction to set in?"

"Convulsions should start in three minutes."

"Enough time. Keep the medicine ready," said Bramara as he perched on Vikram's shoulder. The bird bit his ear gently, till Vikram opened his eyes.

"This is what you will do after you have been given the medicine. Take your awareness to center of your eyebrows. Let's practice it now."

"I am just too tired now. I find it difficult to keep...my eyes...open," mumbled Vikram.

"You have to make an effort. Vikram, remember your quest. Come on."

Bramara looked rattled. He bit Vikram's ears again.

"This is the mantra you will recite...project the awareness along a silver thread into the body of the animal. Keep the thread taut and don't let it snap..."

Kalla could see the huge effort it took from Vikram.

At last, Bramara was convinced that Vikram was ready.

"You may give him the medicine now." Jabala opened the glass vial she carried.

"Open your mouth," she commanded.

Vikram could just manage to coax his lips apart.

Jabala pinch-closed his nostrils hard and his mouth opened. She poured the contents into Vikram's mouth.

"Now! Vikram!" shouted Bramara.

Vikram's eyes closed. His lips started moving. He was obviously reciting something. His muscles tensed and relaxed. His eyes opened wide. Ponni could see that his eyes had stopped moving. *Oh my God, he is dead,* she thought.

Kalla ran to Vikram and felt for Vikram's pulse. There was none. He looked up at Dwipada who nodded.

"Yes, he is dead," said Dwipada.

CHAPTER THIRTY-FOUR
GATES OF MANDALA

Ponni's eyes caught a movement on the side. She saw the pig, which had lain dead till then, twitching and moving, with its eyes open. Ponni thought of fitting an arrow to her bow.

"NO, DON'T!" Dwipada's voice rang out.

Ponni saw that the pig tried to cover its face with its forelegs.

"That's Vikram in the pig's body," Dwipada continued, "Bramara taught Vikram the technique of 'koodu vittu koodu'—the ability of the soul to leave one's body and possess a dead one."

After a while, Dwipada inspected the animal.

"Now, you can get back to your body," he whispered into its ear.

The pig stopped twitching.

"What am I?" was the first thing Vikram said when he got up. No one answered.

They had ridden for several miles past the valley. The forest had thinned out. Thorny bushes and anthills dotted the landscape. Occasionally, a lone areca nut tree stuck out incongruously.

"Have you ever tried climbing an areca nut tree?" Kalla asked Vikram.

"Oh, they are dead easy to climb," said Vikram.

"Yes, but have you tried coming down one?"

"Yes, I always jumped down."

"Why can't you climb down?" asked Jabala, joining the conversation.

"Well, it has sharp bristles all the way on its trunk. The bristles point upward. I am sure I can climb one now. I feel quite strong. Strangely, I feel stronger than I have ever felt before," said Vikram.

"It's the effect of the drug," said Jabala, "It has detoxifying and rejuvenating properties. The only reason we don't administer it more often is its near-fatal side-effects."

"You mean, if you don't die from it, you live longer," said Kalla.

"In fact, it is reputed to have other properties as well. It strengthens your will power and concentration."

"Why didn't you give me the drug as soon as the ghosts got out?" Vikram queried.

"You were so weak that the convulsions would have killed you even before the drug started working."

They heard a metallic sound before they saw the image.

"Welcome, welcome," it said.

Dwipada was the first to react. "Pisacha, in person! What an honor."

Pisacha's image looked around.

"I see that you have survived the journey through the valley. Or have you? Let me count."

His eyes swept over the group rapidly.

"A pity. All of you appear whole. But being your host, I think I should welcome you, even if not quite in person. You can see that I am so transparent in what I do that you can literally see through me. Ha, ha...you are not laughing. It's okay. Nobody laughs anymore at my jokes, except maybe Abhishtu. I am getting sidetracked. I just wanted to let you know that you are welcome to my little kingdom." He paused.

"How generous," muttered Dwipada.

"Yes, I am known for it. However, there are limits. We have a rather quaint custom in my little country. I am afraid you may have to submit to it. It is rather simple. You just have to get through the concentric walls that surround my castle."

"The walls are impregnable. There is, however, an entry point at each wall, where you have to undergo an ordeal. Any one of you may take the test individually or attempt it together as a group. You pass through those walls and you are my guest."

"With effort you may squeeze out oil from a stone; you may even drink up water from a desert mirage. You may wander hither and thither and find a rabbit with horns. But it is impossible to change the attitude of a fool, well entrenched in his idiocy." quoted Bana.

"That was nice," said Pisacha, "I presume there is a point to it."

"Return the Chintamani and we will go our way," said Dwipada.

"Ooo, a bargain! I love it. Cross the hurdles and maybe we can all sit down and talk about it," said Pisacha.

Vikram placed his hand on his sword.

Pisacha's eyes fell on Vikram's hand. He pointed his wand at Vikram.

"I see the tattooed conch and wheel. You must be the youth named Vikram I have heard so much about. Of course, if you wish, you can spend the rest of your life slashing at my image. I did hear you didn't have much between the ears. Now I realize how true it is."

Vikram stood staring as the image flickered and disappeared. He lowered his sword. Bramara emerged from behind Dwipada.

"Why did you hide?" asked Ponni.

"I don't want Pisacha to know I am part of this party. I can be the surprise element," said Bramara.

The hills and the forest had given way to level land, with only a few trees around. At a distance, they saw smoke spiraling up beyond the high elevation of the land. From the top of the rise, they could see the walled city below in the predawn light.

"Mandala!" said Dwipada who rode at the front.

Even from a distance, it was an imposing sight. Vikram saw the concentric walls and a central structure that stood out from the others.

"What a building!" Bana remarked. "Take away the interconnecting bridges between the towers, make the towers round instead of square, build the whole thing of white marble, add a reflecting pool or two, add some trees...it would make a great mausoleum."

"Look," said Asadu, pointing to the road.

"What do you mean?" asked Vikram. "There is nothing to see. No traffic at all."

"That's what I mean. There is no traffic anywhere."

In sharp contrast to the central building, they saw a dilapidated building with thatched roof outside the walled city. The walls of the building reached only half way up to the roof, as its top half had broken down. The road leading up to it was full of potholes and boulders.

"I wonder what that could be for."

"There seems to be a large stable behind. It looks like an inn," said Bramara.

"We will leave the horses there," said Dwipada.

As they entered the run-down building, a strong smell of wet hay and dung greeted them.

"This feels like heaven," said Uchchi.

"Yes," said Chetak. "If there is one on earth, this is it, this is it, this is it."

"ANYONE THERE?" called out Asadu.

A young boy in rags came out through an arched doorway.

"We would like to meet the owner," said Asadu.

"What for? What do you want to know? I can tell you all you want to know," said the boy.

"How much to look after all these horses for a couple of days?" asked Asadu.

"Depends on where you are going."

"We are going to Pisacha Pinda's castle. Why should that make a difference to your charges?"

"If you are going to the castle, the upkeep is free. There is a condition though. If you don't return in three days, the owner gets to keep the horses."

"That's really strange," observed Asadu.

"It's simple. If you are going to the castle, my boss figures you are not going to return. So we get all these horses for free. If you do return, it means that the dreaded Pisacha has been defeated. My boss has some close relatives stuck inside the castle. He figures if they get liberated, what the hell, that's payment enough."

"I would like to inspect the place before we decide."

"Who said that?" the boy looked around.

"Can't you see me? I am standing right in front of you." Chetak's voice showed annoyance.

The boy saw Chetak and paled.

"You...were you the one talking?"

"Chetak, just shut up," said Dwipada. "We don't have a choice here."

"Would you look at a gift horse in the mouth?" asked Bana.

"We agree to your terms," Dwipada told the boy with an air of finality.

"Not that I don't like this place. I just like to have some options," grumbled Chetak to Uchchi as they were led away.

After leaving the horses, the group walked single file along a narrow trail that led down to the castle.

CHAPTER THIRTY-FIVE

TESTING TIMES

Vikram gaped at the huge outer wall of Mandala. A full fifteen meters high, he thought. It was built of large granite blocks that gleamed black in the morning light. Walking further, the group stopped at two enormous brass gates. Two guards stood in front of them, with their backs to each other. They were in white armor and their helmets had white plumes on them. Each held a long lance in one hand and a shield in the other.

"Knights, surely," said Bana. "But where are the knaves? Where are the ones with black leather jackets, leggings, a skullcap and a black patch over one of the eyes?"

"If you were a knave, you wouldn't advertise the fact, would you?" reasoned Kalla.

A notice was displayed prominently between the two gates. Ponni read it aloud.

"Beware ye, all who wish to enter here. The step once taken cannot be undone. You have to choose the right (which may actually be the left) gate to enter. If you choose the wrong gate, you will be instantly obliterated. If you choose the right one, you have earned the right to proceed to the next level. One of the guards is a true knight and always tells the truth and the other is a knave who always lies. You are allowed to ask one of the guards one question and choose the gate based on the answer. Don't be fooled by appearances.

Signed -

One of the two guards"

"It is like poetry," said Asadu.

"That's rubbish. That was entirely in prose," said Jabala.

"Well, I don't understand poetry. Since I do not understand this, I thought quite naturally..."

"Hah, I will tell you what poetry is. You know what a haiku is?" asked Dwipada.

"A high-level plot to dethrone the king?" Ponni hazarded a guess.

"It is a form of Eastern poetry," said Bana with a superior air.

"That's right. Here's a rare example. A very rare one. A *guru*-brother taught me this—"

"Thunder booms.
The swallow spreads its white speckled wings;
Without concern.
And flies away."

"What does that mean?" Bana burst out. "Also a haiku is supposed to be exactly seventeen syllables long. This one is far too long."

"How perceptive," said Dwipada. "This is exactly why it is rare."

Vikram was getting restive. "Can we concentrate on the job at hand?"

"This is going to be tough. We don't know if the guard who has written the sign is truthful or not." Asadu looked concerned.

"Actually that is not a problem. It is quite simple. If the guard who has signed it is a liar, he could not have signed off as one of the guards. Therefore, the board must be telling the truth. Making the correct choice is going to be a tough one," said Vikram.

Bana looked happy. "I love logic gates..."

Vikram's patience reached a limit. He drew his sword.

"I will get the truth out of this guard."

"Hold it, I can handle this," Bana snapped his fingers.

"Go ahead, we trust you," said Madavi.

She looked around and was met with fixed stares. Vikram sheathed his sword.

"I like the guard to my left. A big-made fellow. He has an honest face." Bana walked up to the guard and said something to him. Vikram watched from a distance. He saw a strange expression on the guard's face. Soon, the guard's face turned purple and a choked 'yes' was heard.

"This way," said Bana.

They all trooped in through the open gate. As they passed the guard, Vikram noticed he still had the strangled expression.

"Is he the one who tells the truth?" asked Asadu.

"I am Dubaku, Abhishtu's nephew," said the guard.

"You look smart," said Asadu.

"So my mother always told me," said Dubaku. "She always told me that I resemble my uncle but look much better than him. He is squint-eyed, you know."

"I wonder what would have happened if we had chosen the wrong gate," said Asadu.

Dubaku pointed to the guard tower inside. The slits on the tower were bristling with arrows.

They crossed the gate and walked along a cobbled path.

"What happened, did you stab him with your pen or something? And was he a liar?" asked Vikram, as he turned toward Bana.

Bana ignored Vikram and shrugged his shoulders. "I don't know."

"What do you mean, you don't know?"

"It is not relevant whether or not he was a liar." Bana looked like a playwright who was being introduced to the audience by a narrator at the hundredth performance. "What I asked him was this: 'If I asked you if this was the right way, what would you say?'"

Seeing that, Asadu still wore a puzzled look, Bana explained further.

"Let us assume he was a true knight. Then he would have said 'Yes', if it were the right way and 'No', if it weren't. One could get the right way simply by following what he said."

"On the other hand, let us assume he were a knave, and the way he pointed to was really the right way. Then he would have wanted to say 'No'. Since the question was about what he would have said, he would want to lie about what he wanted to say and said 'Yes'. In either case, all you needed to do was to follow what the guard said."

Asadu looked at him admiringly. "I still can't figure this out."

"What if he were a knave and this was the wrong choice?" Kalla asked.

"I didn't think through, I guess," said Bana.

"C'mon," said Vikram, "two negatives make a positive, didn't you know that?"

"No, I did not," said Asadu, as they entered a tunnel.

CHAPTER THIRTY-SIX

UMLOCHA

One down. Seven more to go. Vikram was keyed up with excitement as they walked along the tunnel. They made their way in silence; their footsteps echoed in the tunnel and made any conversation difficult. Finally, they stepped into an oblong room. It was lit with a torch burning at the far end. Heaped to one side were skulls and other human bones. Some of them still had pieces of flesh adhering to them.

Hanging over a curtained doorway was a board that read, "BEFORE YE ENTER."

Jabala moved closer to the board and in the flickering light, she read the fine print on it aloud.

"One and only one of you should pass through these curtains. If that person comes back alive, you may all pass on to the next level."

"Cryptic, isn't it?" said Jabala.

Dwipada rotated his head about a horizontal axis centered approximately on his nose, in a pattern that was neither a nod nor a shake. Before anyone could react, Vikram moved the curtains aside and stepped into a room beyond.

It took a while for Vikram's eyes to adapt to the semi-darkness of the room. The room was dominated by a bed decorated with strings of orange *sampangi* flowers. The bed had rose petals strewn on it. Vikram sat on the bed. It felt very soft. He was certain that the mattress was made of silk cotton from the *ilavam* tree. He sat at the edge as his sword came in the way.

As Vikram looked around, he saw a figure at the far end of the room. The figure came nearer. It was that of a beautiful woman. Her beauty was beyond any words of description. *Face pleasing as the full moon, complexion like that of a yellow lotus. Eyes large and beautiful like a gazelle's.* She wore a string of off-white pearls matching her white silk sari that hung over breasts that looked like the forehead of an elephant. An armlet and a stack of gold bangles. The grace of a swan. A jeweled girdle worn low. Above the girdle, three perfect creases of flesh. This decided it. She was a Padmini! A perfect example of the highest form of womanhood. Just as it was described in the *Fragrant Lawn*. Her anklets tinkled as she walked toward him. Her teeth flashed white like bleached pearls and when she spoke, it was in a husky voice.

"You have come, my lover."

"No...yes, I see what you mean. I am here."

"Ah, such facility with words. You have come in response to my ardent prayers, have you not?"

"No, actually..."

It was then that he saw her feet were not touching the ground, which gave her the graceful glide of a swan. He put his hand on the hilt of his sword.

"Why are you playing with that thing at your waist? Stop doing that. Relax and enjoy."

Her voice was like a *yazh* wielded by expert hands. Her hips swayed like a palm tree in a strong breeze. Her lips were pouting, moist and invitingly open.

She held out her arms. The perfume of sandal, *attar* and musk wafting across made Vikram giddy. He lowered his gaze. He saw the way the folds of her sari revealed her well-rounded calf muscles, her ankles and...*her feet pointed the other way.*

Stardust tore away from his eyes in big clumps.

"Stop! I know who...what you are. You are a succubus, a Mohini Pisasu, aren't you? You come any nearer and the sword will taste your blood." She stopped moving forward.

"I am just a defenseless maiden who is hoping to be your lover."

She sighed deeply. Her bosom heaved, sending the pearls deep into her cleavage. Vikram's hand tightened around his sword.

The Mohini's doe-like eyes widened. "It's not possible. No one has ever resisted my charm..."

"Unless?"

"How did you know I was going to say 'unless'? Unless you have been subjected to an extremely risky form of drug therapy."

"Which is exactly what I have been subjected to, Mohini."

"Then you must be..."

"Come on, I haven't got all day. Just show me the way out of this place, and move aside. Or should I run you through and get it over with?"

"Wait. Pl...Please listen to my story." The catch in her voice didn't seem feigned.

"All right, go on. Quickly. But don't leave out the interesting bits."

"My name is Umlocha. I was one of the divine danseuses at the court of Indra, the king of gods. The principal *apsaras* in his court were Urvasi, Ramba, Tillottama and Menaka. These *apsaras* always won praises and gifts from Indra. Who do you think got all the plum assignments? Not me. They were allowed to have paid public performances and they kept half the proceeds, off the top. They landed all the cushy jobs. For instance, Urvasi and Tilottama were the first choice when it came to disturbing old men from their penances. Imagine seducing an old man who hasn't had sex in a hundred years. I could have done it merely by exposing a toenail."

"I can well imagine," said Vikram.

"Indra used to have dancing contests every year and the winner was promoted to be one of the principal *apsaras*. A mortal, usually a well-known king from the earth, judged these contests. King Vikrama was the adjudicator one particular year. I was desperate to win. So naturally, the night before the contest, I visited Vikrama. Before I could even bat my eyelids at Vikrama, Indra was there."

"Trying to influence the judge, I see," he said. He then proceeded to deliver a lecture on ethics and morality.

"That's when I lost my cool. I pointed out instances when he hadn't been a paragon of rectitude. Perhaps, I should not have referred to the time he had to run away and hide because his body was ridden with a thousand vaginas due to a curse."

"Not very diplomatic, I guess," muttered Vikram.

"He cursed me. I was to roam as a Mohini Pisasu on earth, a succubus preying on young and the old alike. I waited for the mandatory redemption clause. Finally, he spelled it out. More of that a little later."

Vikram was getting drawn into the story.

"You know how it is. Some women like to smoke a *chillum* after sex. I usually ate my partner. For a while, I was going from place to place hungry for men. I was not averse to a few women on the side; I was a bi-pisasu. Then, one day, Pisacha found me and offered me a permanent place and an abundant food supply. He fed me every day, whether or not there was a challenger at the gates. I, of course, prefer to eat a challenger because I think things are a little sweeter when you have earned them."

She paused. Vikram looked at the *apsara*. She seemed soft and vulnerable.

"So, Umlocha, what was the redemption clause?"

"This is what Indra told me—'Since you have tried to seduce King Vikram, you will be freed from this curse when you try to seduce a man by name Vikram when he tries to kill you.'"

"My name is Vikram," said Vikram.

"My savior. At last, my redemption is at hand. Please run through me with your sword," pleaded the Mohini.

"Well..." said Vikram, "I don't normally raise my sword against women."

Before he could decide on a course of action, Umlocha jerked his hand upward and fell on his sword. When things transform magically, there is an instant of transition when there is only emptiness. Even before the sword touched her, there was a moment of utter darkness.

When the darkness cleared, a distinctly different woman stood before him. She wore a different shade of eye makeup and was clad in white.

Also a Padmini.

"Well..." he said.

"What now, mortal?" Umlocha's voice sounded imperious.

"Aren't you forgetting something?"

"Explain yourself."

"Aren't you supposed to thank me profusely for saving you from the curse, and aren't you supposed to give, sorry, bequeath a divine object that will help me in my quest?"

"No," said Umlocha, "that's only in fairy tales. Let me go."

"Not so fast," said Vikram. "At least tell me what dangers lie ahead for us."

"All right. Next you have to confront Kumalla, a great wrestler, perhaps the greatest of all times. He keeps the key to the next level on his person. You have to defeat him to move forward."

Umlocha disappeared.

CHAPTER THIRTY-SEVEN

THE WRESTLER

It had been over an hour since Vikram stepped behind the curtains. Ponni felt nervous. She paced up and down.

"Stop acting like a cat about to have kittens," Jabala admonished her, to no apparent effect.

"Perhaps we should see what is happening inside. If Vikram has been eaten up by a demon or something, we can at least perform his last rites," said Asadu.

Ponni winced at this.

"Let's wait a little longer," said Dwipada.

"How much longer?" Ponni's eyes were drawn to the heap of skeletons.

Suddenly, Dwipada shouted, "I CANNOT WAIT ANY LONGER. WE WILL GO IN. I WILL REDUCE THIS PALACE TO ASHES, USING EVERY BIT OF MY POWER OF TAPASYA."

"There should be no need for it," said Vikram as he came out through the curtains.

"You are alright!" said Ponni.

Jabala let out a collective sigh of relief for the entire group.

"What happened? I am glad you didn't get eaten up." Asadu parted the curtains and peered into the room. He whistled.

"That is a bridal setup, if ever there was one."

"Oh, nothing much," said Vikram with exaggerated casualness. "There was this Mohini—"

"—Mohini Pisasu!" echoed Asadu.

"—Who actually turned out to be an *apsara*."

"—An *apsara*!" It was Asadu again.

"—Who had been cursed by Indra," said Vikram and looking at Asadu, he quickly added, "and don't shout Indra!"

Asadu looked back at him innocently.

Dwipada looked like a sage who had something on his mind as they all trooped into the room.

Ponni looked at the bed and the floral decoration.

"Was she very beautiful?" Her voice was completely devoid of expression.

"Yes, of course. She was a regular Padmini."

"Oh, wow," said Kalla.

"And who would this Padmini be?" Ponni had her hands on her hips and her eyes were flashing fire.

"The *Fragrant Lawn*—" Vikram began.

"She is a character in a book. An ugly woman inside and out." Kalla came to Vikram's rescue.

"I wish we knew what lies ahead," said Bana, his jowls quivering. "What exotic twists of fate await me, what savage savageries of cruel parting I have to endure..."

"What rubbish! Anyway that reminds me—" started Vikram.

"Sorry, I got carried away. That's from my play. Go on."

"The Mohini said something more. She said we would have to face Kumalla, a wrestler who will have a key to enter the next level."

"Hmm...and we should beat him to get to the next level." From the way Kalla said it, Vikram could see he had been thinking.

"Well, um...er...regarding the Mohini," Dwipada began. No one spoke. "I was wondering if you had anything, you know, to do with her."

"Well, I almost ran her through with my sword, or rather she fell on my sword." Ponni looked happy and Dwipada seemed relieved.

"If you had anything physical to do with her, you would have been turned into a *pisasu* yourself." Just to make sure, Dwipada stole a quick glance at Vikram's feet and was satisfied. They left the room in silence, in search of the next gate.

The wrestler was waiting for them in a lighted alcove. His upper body was bare and glistening with oil. Muscles rippled through his body in large wavelets. Occasionally, he struck his thighs with his large fists, calling out challenges.

"You must be Kumalla. We are supposed to overpower you if we have to get any further. Am I right?" Vikram said.

Kumalla stepped out of the alcove. Vikram noticed that his canines were razor sharp.

"Don't you muscle into my speaking part," said Kumalla. "I will say my piece. I am Kumalla the wrestler. The strongest and the wiliest on the planet. I challenge you to single combat. If you beat me, you may pass through this door behind me."

"And you think we are frightened by your filed teeth?" asked Vikram.

"Oh," said Kumalla. "That is purely functional. I eat my enemies."

The stab of fear that Vikram felt on seeing the canines now threatened to disembowel him by hacking and slashing within.

"So you want one of us fight you?" asked Kalla, stepping forward. "I volunteer."

Dwipada's eyes widened. Madavi looked at him in admiration. Asadu and Bana were visibly impressed. Vikram objected. "No, no, I cannot allow you to put yourself in danger."

"...You mistake me. I nominate Bana," said Kalla, pushing Bana forward.

"Huh?" said Bana.

Before Vikram could react, Kalla spoke again.

"What would the rules be, Kumalla? I presume standard wrestling federation rules apply."

"Anything is fine, as long as I am allowed to beat you to a pulp and eat you afterwards," said Kumalla, licking his lips.

"We don't have much time," said Kalla. "So we have to speed things up a bit."

"So I eat him and then fight with him?" asked Kumalla.

"That wasn't funny. This is what we will do. The match will have only two rounds. It will start with one of you in the defensive position on his hands and knees on the mat. For the second round, the roles will reverse. Standard points for throws, takedowns, fall and reversals apply. Whoever gets more points wins. Now do you want to toss to see who should start with the defensive position?"

"It will be no fun if I throw this boy and trample him to death in the first minute. I will take the defensive position. No need to toss. Woohoo!" Kumalla said, slapping his thighs.

"Woohoo," replied Bana in a rather low voice.

"Wait. Will the non-combatants clear the ring please?" Kalla herded everyone away from the contestants toward a locked door.

"Don't try to slip out," said Kumalla. "It's locked. Even I cannot open it without a key."

Kalla approached Bana ostensibly to check him. He whispered some instructions to Bana as he took away his scriber and palm leaves that he carried around his waist.

"Are you sure I can't raise both my hands, throw my head back and shout...'Thus we defeat you, minions of Pisacha'?" Bana whispered.

"No, just stick to the script," said Kalla.

Bana nodded, muttering something.

Kalla checked Kumalla perfunctorily.

"Are you ready to start?"

Kumalla took the 'down' position, on his knees and hands. Kalla moved him around till he faced away from the exit. Bana took his position with his left hand around Kumalla's waist and for some strange reason, he kept running his hands over Kumalla's back.

"Hey, what are you doing," shouted Kumalla. "You are facing the wrong way. And stop sitting on me. Amateurs," he muttered under his breath when there was no reply.

Meanwhile, Kalla was busy. He had unlocked the exit door. He winked at Vikram and gestured to the others to file out of the room.

On Kalla's signal, Bana wiped his hands on the soles of Kumalla's feet.

"Hey, what are you doing? That tickles," bellowed Kumalla.

"Now!" shouted Kalla.

Bana got up with an effort and ran towards the exit.

By then, Kumalla knew something was wrong and he turned around. He got up with a shout, only to slip and fall down, as his soles were smeared with oil.

Bana and Kalla left last, locking the door behind them.

CHAPTER THIRTY-EIGHT

THE FISH

"How did you open the door, Kalla?" There was admiration in Madavi's voice.

"Oh, I opened it with a key," said Kalla.

"I know, but how did you happen to have the right one?"

"Well, I sort of abstracted it from Kumalla when I patted him down at the start of the contest," said Kalla.

After walking through a dark corridor, they entered a brightly lit room. Vikram shaded his eyes with his hand to see. The room was small, with a high ceiling and a pool in the middle. Suspended from the ceiling above the pool was a wooden wheel, no more than a handspan in diameter, spinning lazily in counter-clockwise direction. Above the wheel was a small wooden fish, hardly a couple of inches long. The fish moved around in a clockwise direction but not in a single plane.

The bottom of the pool was embedded with a large number of tiny mirrors, each set at different angle to the base. Each mirror reflected the spinning wheel and the fish.

Ponni looked around for a signboard—there was none. The only object around was a hollow cone near a large chest to one side of the pool.

"Do you think the cone is for drinking water from the pool?" Bana picked it up and was examining it closely when the cone came to life.

"Testing, testing, testing," it said. "Sorry, this is the first time the apparatus is being activated. If you have come this far, you are probably a worthy contender. What you have to do is to take the bow out from the chest, fit the single arrow provided and shoot the fish through the wheel. Oh, one more thing, you can't look at it directly while shooting, only at its reflections in the mirrors in the pool. Ah yes, you have to do it within a minute of picking up the bow from the box. You only have one chance. Is that clear? Anyway, let me repeat the instructions. What you have to do..."

The instruction droned on but Asadu and Vikram ignored it. They rushed toward the box. Asadu kicked the lid open. Vikram reached inside to take the bow out and after a couple of initial heaves, drew his hand back with an expression of dismay.

"It's heavy," he exclaimed, breathing hard.

Asadu and Vikram then placed their hands below the ends of the bow.

"NOW TOGETHER...AILASA," shouted Vikram and both tried to lift the bow simultaneously.

The bow did not budge.

It was a simple unornamented bow, already strung. It was made of iron.

"Vikram, do it the other way." Asadu and Vikram were about to switch places when Dwipada stopped them.

"No, that's not what I meant. Vikram, use your power!" Vikram centered himself.

"A tad to the left," said Dwipada. Vikram did so. He, his energy and the bow were now one. The bow rose from the box on its own and floated gently toward the pool and hovered over it.

"Your time starts NOW," said the cone.

Vikram looked once at the wheel and the fish. He then looked at the reflection in a single tile at the bottom of the pool. He grabbed the bow and held it rock steady. He was about to fit the arrow to the bowstring when Dwipada cried out, "Stop, let Ponni do it. She is a better shot."

Ponni took the bow with a smirk. She fitted the arrow and just as she was about to draw it using both her hands, Bana let out a howl of disappointment. Large drops of water from the wheel overhead fell on the surface of the pool, creating ripples and distorting the images. Ponni did not seem to notice. Her head was bent in concentration. She released the arrow. The next moment, a 'ping' was heard as the arrow pierced the fish. A grinding noise followed. A circular door on the roof opened and a rope ladder dropped from it, revealing the entrance to the next level.

"I wonder what would have happened," Kalla remarked as he prepared to climb the ladder, "if the arrow had not hit the fish."

"If you hadn't succeeded, the wheel would have come crashing down and exploded," said the cone. "It is packed with sharp iron pieces. None of you would have been alive."

Vikram was still flush with anger. He closed his eyes and gestured. The bow bent into a D, then into a teardrop and beyond, and shattered. Ponni looked around for something to vent her anger upon. She saw the cone lying around and kicked it hard.

The cone said, "Ow," and went up several feet in the air. It came crashing to the ground and lay silent.

"That feels good!" said Ponni and Vikram simultaneously.

CHAPTER THIRTY-NINE

THE TRUE FLOWER

"I wonder how you managed to hit the fish even though the surface was disturbed by water droplets." Bana looked puzzled.

"That wasn't a problem," said Ponni. "I had already formed an image in my mind and believe it or not, I closed my eyes before I released the arrow."

"With the wheel rotating and the fish moving crazily, how did you ever hit the target?"

"Oh, that was smart," said Vikram. "Ponni must have realized that the fish wasn't actually moving in an irregular way. It was moving along a simple harmonographic locus..."

Seeing that Bana's eyes were glazing over, Vikram hastened to explain.

"That's a combination of motions in mutually perpendicular directions. Anyway, it wouldn't have been easy to figure out where the fish was going to be at every instant of time."

"Oh, it wasn't too difficult," said Ponni. "I just concentrated on the eye of the fish and shot at it." She paused a little before she continued on.

"What made it difficult was that the fish did not have an eye painted on it. I had to imagine one and shoot at it."

They emerged into the open. The wall in front of them stretched to a great distance in both directions. It looked as though a horizontal pink stripe had been painted on a portion of the curved wall. Vikram and Kalla ran ahead of the others. The pink stripe resolved into a row of identical-looking pink lotuses in metallic vases.

There were nine of them on a ledge jutting out of the wall. Resting on it was a signboard. Kalla read it aloud, even as the others caught up with them.

"Pick out the only natural flower among these. Do not touch until you make your choice. What you touch first will be deemed to be your choice. Once you have chosen, carry the vase to the circular platform to your left. Place it on the matching depression at the center. All members of the party should then stand on that platform and await further instructions/developments."

"I would rather have instructions than developments," Vikram muttered to himself. He looked around and saw the circular platform made of polished stone.

"Hmm..." Jabala looked thoughtful. "The texture will probably give it away, but you are not allowed to touch."

"Don't tell me we are not allowed to taste it either." Bana didn't realize that he had spoken aloud.

"I know." Asadu spoke excitedly in a shrill voice. "The scent. You can't mimic the natural scent of a lotus." Almost immediately his face fell. "But I can't do this. Having been a washing stone most of my life, my sense of smell is partially and permanently damaged. Everything now smells of unwashed clothes."

"I am trained to do this. I can make out even faint smells." Madavi approached the ledge with her hands clasped behind her to avoid touching the flowers by accident. She first took a short sniff followed by a much longer one. She repeated this for all the flowers. She stepped back, disappointment writ on her face.

"They all smell of jasmine. They must have been sprayed with a scent. This has masked the natural odor."

Dwipada cleared his throat. "I have an idea. On the day of the Swati Asterism, when a raindrop falls into an oyster, it becomes a pearl. When it falls on burning embers, it disappears as steam—"

"The point being?" interjected Bramara who had been sitting on Dwipada's shoulders with a bored look.

"Wait, I am getting there. When a raindrop falls on a lotus leaf, it shines like a pearl." He looked around in triumph. "Don't you get it? Lotus leaves are hydrophobic. All you have to do is..."

"What you are forgetting, revered one, is we have only the flowers and not the leaves."

"Hmm..." Dwipada's face showed no emotion beneath the beard.

"Don't worry. If you have all finished trying, I will find the real flower in a moment." Bramara, who managed to look smug all the while, transformed into a bee with a faint 'ting'. In a moment, he changed back. "The third from the right. Kalla, bring it to the platform."

"You didn't even go near it!" Vikram looked at Bramara with amazement.

"It was nothing," said Bramara. "I have to teach you a bit of science before I can explain it to you. You have seen a rainbow, haven't you?"

"Indra's bow. Yes," said Bana, "for some reason, my heart leaps up every time I see one."

"What colors have you seen on a rainbow?"

"Well," said Vikram with closed eyes, "red, orange, yellow, green, blue, indigo and violet, in that order." He opened his eyes again.

"Good. There are colors beyond violet and are invisible to the human eye. Not so for a bee. As a bee I can see far beyond violet. And all natural flowers have come-hither markings on them, clearly marked out in beyond-violet."

"Wow, Bramara. You haven't taught me the magic of transformation. I am also curious about the 'ting' I heard when you changed into a bee."

"The 'ting' wasn't really necessary. It was for artistic reasons. And humans cannot transform by magic."

"What are you then?"

"A sentient being," said Bramara as they made their way to the circular stone platform. Kalla was the last to get onto the platform. He placed the vase in the depression in the middle of the platform. It fitted in with a click. There was a low whirring sound and a section of the wall opened up revealing a path.

CHAPTER FORTY
COINS AND BALANCE

The path led to a covered enclosure with three doors at the far end. Two doors to the sides were marked 'EXIT' in large letters, with *To the next level*' written in much smaller font beneath one of the signs and '*Permanent*' below the other. The door in the middle was slightly ajar and the sign on it read 'STORE'. A man in a turban and a luxurious mustache sat cross-legged on the floor in the middle of the enclosure. A weighing scale with two concave pans lay on the floor. The pans, though made of iron, were rust-free and gleaming. The crossbeam and chain links rested on the pans.

The man grinned at them, showing teeth and large expanses of gum where they ought to have been teeth.

"Wow," said Bana, "this is fantastic. They are selling sweets. I would love to buy some."

"Don't be silly," said Kalla. "Could be, they weigh everyone and only the ones below a certain weight are allowed to enter."

"Shut up! Let's find out what he has to say." Vikram strode up to the man.

"This is a test," said the man, "or rather two tests—the first one is taken by one person and the second by another. Are you ready for the easier one?"

"Yes," said Vikram.

"Let me get the coins for the test," said the man. He went into the store and returned with a handful of shiny coins.

Everyone crowded around him to get a better look. He held out his open hands.

"Here are nine coins, one of which is a fake and a little lighter than the others. You have to identify which of these is false in minimum number of weighings. In fact, even I do not know which one is the fake. For this test there are no external weights and you can only weigh coins against other coins. You can use this sensitive balance here. You may decide which of you is going to try. If I do better using lesser number of weighing, you will lose more than a game. Your lives are at stake."

Bana's brow was furrowed and it kept going up and down indicating frenetic mental activity. Vikram stared vacantly. He too was lost in thought.

After a while, Bana's brow cleared. He took a step forward and turned, swishing his robes to face his comrades.

"Friends, I, Bana, have solved this problem. I can do this in just..."

He looked around to let his words sink in. "I can do it in just four weighings. I repeat, four."

"Wow, how would you do that?" asked Jabala.

"Simple," said Bana. "Take the coins in pairs and weigh one against another. At each step, if they weigh the same, they have to be genuine coins. If one is lighter, you have the fake coin in that set. One more weighing with one coin on each pan will reveal the fake coin. If, in all four steps, you have equal weights, the ninth coin is the fake one."

Bana bowed to all around.

"That gives me an idea," said Ponni. "I think I can do it in three weighings."

"That's one weighing too many," said Vikram. "The minimum number of weighings is just two. Imagine you had only three coins and you had to find which one is lighter. The answer is obvious. You weigh one of the coins against another and you find the lighter coin. If the pans balance, the third coin is the fake."

"But we have nine coins," said Bana.

"So, you divide them into three groups of three coins each. In one weighing, you find the lighter group. Use the same method to find the lighter coin within the group by weighing one of the coins against the other."

"I can do it in one weighing," said Kalla.

"That's mathematically impossible," said Vikram.

"Just watch me," said Kalla, "and learn."

He turned around, facing away from the group and bent down for a moment.

"Praying, are you? You will need it." The man in the turban commented.

Kalla turned back again, strode towards the balance, squatted and picked it up by the hook on its beam, letting one of the pans rest on his thigh. He then added four coins to each of the pans, keeping the ninth aside. As he lifted the hook a little, the pans were perfectly balanced. He took out the ninth coin in triumph and bowed to the man with the mustache. "There you have it—the fake."

He then quickly made all the coins into one pile and handed them over to the man.

The man was unfazed. "You took a great risk, my boy," he said. "That was just a fluke. In the next test, you can't count on dumb luck. Let me get a few more things needed for the second test." He turned back toward the door marked 'STORE'.

Vikram, who had been holding his breath all the while, let it out with a whoosh. "You were just dumb lucky. You put all our lives at risk. Do you know what kind of a chance you took? What would you have done if the pans hadn't balanced? There was almost a ninety percent probability of that."

"Hey Vikram, hold on. Can I have some trust, please? I took no risk, and luck had very little to do with it." He looked around to check if the man was still busy inside the store and with a flourish, he pushed up his pantaloons and exposed his legs just above the knee.

Kalla ignored the whispered "Oo, nice legs," from Madavi. A small round stone was strapped above his knee. "A magnet. Even if the pans did not balance, the magnet would hold the pan to my knee and make the pans appear balanced."

Madavi gave him an admiring glance.

The man returned with four bags. He emptied the contents of three of them on the floor in separate piles. The fourth one contained standard weights. "These three heaps contain fake and real coins. Some of the counterfeit coins may be lighter and some may be heavier than the normal coins. However, a single heap has only one type of coin, which may be genuine, lighter or heavier."

"Is there one heap of each type?" asked Vikram.

"Not necessarily. All of them may be of the same type or different, or two of them may be similar. Anything is possible. However, the genuine coins weigh exactly ten *tolas*. The fake coins differ by exactly one *tola*. You have to determine the type of heap with the minimum number of weighings."

"Hmm..." said Vikram, "Bana, can you give me a palm leaf and your scriber. I need to work things out. There are twenty-seven possibilities."

"I have heard of a similar problem," said Madavi. "there were ten heaps and one of them had fake coins. The solution was to pick one from the first pile, two from the second and so on, with ten from the tenth and weigh them together."

"That won't work in this case because the fake heaps may contain either a lighter or a heavier coin," Vikram said without looking up from the notes he was making on his leaf. "But you have given me an idea. Just give me five minutes to put something down on this leaf."

Vikram was busy writing something down. At last, he looked up. "I have got it," he said.

He then took one coin from the first pile, three from the second and nine from the third pile and placed them on one of the pans. He then started adding weights on the other pan till the pans were balanced.

He counted the weights.

"One hundred twenty-five *tolas*," he said.

He looked at the leaf with his scribbled notes.

"What's that?" asked Kalla.

Vikram showed him the leaf.

"I can't make head or tail of this," said Kalla.

"Just a moment," said Vikram. He ran his finger down the rows of numbers on the leaf till he came to the ninth row. He read out—"Plus, plus, minus."

He now turned to the mustached man. "That means that the first two piles are of fake coins that are heavier and the third is a pile with lighter coins."

The turbaned man's mustache seemed to droop a little. "That's right," he said in a low voice. He reached at his waist to pull out a bunch of keys and unlocked the door marked 'EXIT—*to the next level*'.

CHAPTER FORTY-ONE
BLOOD SEED

They stepped out onto a large quadrangle that was open to the sky. There was a curved wall in front of them, which had an opening that looked like an exit. Its floor was paved with cobblestones along the sides to a width of about six feet. Grass grew in the gaps between the stones. Its center was filled with fine sand.

Looks like an arena.

Vikram looked around for a board with instructions. There was none.

A hissing noise revealed an opening in the wall. Vikram's attention was now focused on the opening. A giant of a man in black armor emerged. He held a long broadsword. He was bareheaded and he carried no shield.

"I am Rakta Bija. I challenge you to a sword fight to death. Yours, that is. We initially fight one-on-one. Nominate your first champion, or rather victim."

"What was that?" asked Dwipada, hand cupped to an ear.

"Rakta Bija," said Ponni.

"Blood seed," muttered Dwipada. "A strange name."

"We nominate Vikram, that's me." Vikram drew his curved sword.

Bramara fluttered his wings in agitation.

"Get close," advised Asadu. "He can only thrust or hack with his long blade. He cannot cut."

The combatants moved to the center of the arena. They circled each other warily, each looking for an opening. Bija had his sword out. He swished it around making figures of eight with dazzling speed as though it was not a broadsword but a rapier.

Only amateurs make unnecessary flourishes.

For a moment Vikram thought he had his opponent's measure. He had been taught that it was always a good thing if the enemy underestimates him.

Then came the opponent's rush. Bija brought his sword down in a mighty overhead smash that would have sheared Vikram into two. Vikram stepped aside and let the sword whistle past harmlessly.

Vikram assumed a fighting pose, toes inwards, legs wide apart, back straight and leaning forward.

"Ah, the horse stance!" said Bija. "So you can fight after all."

In a lightning-fast maneuver, Rakta Bija assumed the rider posture and brought the sword down. Vikram moved aside, but not fast enough. A thin line of blood appeared on his left shoulder.

Ponni's hand found its way to her mouth.

"The new strike I taught you," hissed Dwipada.

Vikram's face was grim. Things appeared to happen in slow motion. The momentum of Bija's strike had unbalanced him. Vikram steadied himself, turned side-on to Bija and spread his feet to shoulder width. His knees were flexed slightly; he bent forward with his rear sticking out. He gripped his sword with both hands locked together, with the little finger of his right hand overlapping the space between the index finger and middle finger of his left hand.

"What is this strange heathen move?" shouted the bewildered Bija.

As Vikram waggled his sword, Bija watched mesmerized. Vikram's torso rotated, first his shoulders, then his hips, maintaining his spine angled all the while, left hand straight and true, and wrists cocking naturally on the upswing. The tip of his sword pointed toward Bija.

Then his body uncoiled, beginning with his feet. He lowered his sword, with his arms parallel to the ground.

He held his head still all the while. He was counting in his head—
one, two, three..."

"FOUR!" he shouted out as his wrists released the sword that
became a blur. As the dazed Bija turned his head in a reflex action, the
sword struck the back of his neck. It cut into his spinal cord.

Vikram held his stance for a while, as he had been taught by his
guru. He raised the heel of his right foot and his weight rested on his left
foot.

Most sword fights in history never lasted for more than thirty
seconds. This was no exception. Bija fell, face down.

"I adopted this move from a sport of the future, though I am not
certain why they shout out 'four!'," claimed Dwipada, craning his neck
around to face the rest of the group.

The group was horrified at a scene that played out immediately
after the fall of Bija. Even though Bija's cape absorbed most of the blood
that gushed out, a drop of it fell on the ground. The drop sizzled and
burst, spewing thick smoke. As the group watched in dread, sixteen
Rakta Bijas materialized out of the smoke.

"Now you know why I let you cut me," said one of them and laughed
uproariously.

Dwipada smacked his forehead with the palm of his hand. "Why
didn't I realize this before? Blood-seed—when a drop of blood spills,
more Rakta Bijas emerge."

Fifteen Bijas spread out and soon there was a general melee.

"Make sure you don't spill any blood!" Dwipada shouted out in
warning.

Bana was now facing a Bija.

"Don't look at me," he said, "face the spectators." The Bija was
momentarily distracted and Bana plunged his scriber deep into his
chest, turned around to face a loudly applauding horde of imaginary
spectators.

"Die, knave, as I bury my pen deep into your vitals and kill you. I have now avenged thee all now, my mother, my father, my lover, my brothers, sisters and cousins twice removed..."

He stopped his speech as he saw Jabala looking at him strangely.

"Sorry," he said. "I got carried away. That's a line from one of my plays."

"Why don't you withdraw your pen?" said Jabala sweetly.

The Bija fell, his face contorted.

Asadu managed to keep his foe at bay with some fancy stick work. He made complex arabesques in the air. The trajectory of his sticks was intercepted by some of the Bija's body parts.

Ponni butted her Bija hard in the solar plexus. Kamadenu had taught her this move well. The opponent went down and stayed down. She then turned to another Bija. The divided lower garment that the Bija was wearing made it easier for Ponni to aim. She could almost hear Chetak screaming in her head to 'use the balls'. She kicked. The balls of her feet connected. The Bija fell clutching at his groin.

Bramara flew about, giving advice and encouragement.

Kalla managed to tighten a noose of thin wire around the neck of a Bija. The Bija flailed his arms and grunted and growled. His eyes bulged from the pressure.

Jabala joined Bana. A Bija raised his sword to cut Bana down. Jabala's hand moved with lightning speed. The knife she was holding was a blur as it plunged into his side and came out through the other. The Bija clutched at his form as Jabala busied herself with replacing the tip of the dagger.

Dwipada did not fare so well. For one, he had to use the blunt side of his ax and for another, three Bijas converged on him and were harassing him. He swung it around in a horizontal arc. It was clear he could not hold out much longer. Vikram, who looked around to see how the battle was progressing, noticed that the Rakta Bijas had regrouped in pairs. Each pair was after a single opponent. The situation appeared hopeless.

"Vikram, quick, use the Nagapasa," shouted Bramara.

Vikram bent down and plucked a blade of grass. He closed his eyes, quickly propitiated his ten gods and muttered an invocation to the celestial snake beings—Sesha, Karkotaka and Takshaka. He chanted the final mantra and threw the blade of grass upward.

One thousand snakes appeared from nowhere, hissing and spitting as they sped toward the Bijas. The serpents wound themselves tight around the Bijas. "Jabala, Ponni!" Dwipada called out. "The effect of Nagapasa will not last long. Scratch every Bija's neck with the tip of your poisoned dagger. Make sure you don't puncture a blood vessel. No drop of blood should spill on the ground."

Seeing the women hesitate, Dwipada hastened to assure them, "They are not true living beings. There is no sin in killing them even when they are defenseless."

If Ponni found the task difficult because of her fear of snakes, no one would guess by looking at her beautiful face that betrayed no fear. If anything, it only showed a grim resolve. Jabala executed the job with the smoothness of a professional.

From a distance, Vikram saw a Bija bleeding from a wound to his neck. A drop of blood was about to spill on the ground. He wanted to shout out a warning, but even as he opened his mouth, he knew it was going to be too late.

CHAPTER FORTY-TWO

DUSSAKUNI REPORTS

Pisacha paced up and down in his chamber with his head cast down. Trijada stood unobtrusively on one side.

"ABHISHTU!" he looked up and shouted.

"Yes, boss?" responded Abhishtu, as he entered the chamber.

"Where are they now?"

"Who, boss?"

"Idiot. Obviously, I am talking about Dwipada and his bunch of idiots. Trijada, more wine!"

To do something meekly, you need to hold your head down, have your arms close to the body and not make exaggerated movements. In short, it is an art.

Trijada poured wine meekly from the jar she was holding in one hand and handed the mug to Pisacha.

"All I know is that they have passed through the first gate. My nephew Dubaku reported this, boss." Abhishtu wrung his hands nervously as he said this.

In his peripheral vision, Pisacha could see a short figure in dark robes hesitating to enter the room.

"Dussakuni!" he called out. "Stop dithering! Come in! You have come at the right time. What do you have to report?"

"Like you asked me to, boss, I followed them and overheard their conversation. I took a shortcut after we passed the valley of ghosts and came here directly, boss."

"And...?"

"Found more information about the boy. His name is Vikram. He comes from Orum."

"Orum? How did he manage to get out of the place, I wonder? Continue your report."

"Father is Kuyavan. He calls himself a terracotta artist."

"A potter, you mean?"

"Mother is Durga, an ex-dancer."

"Is Vikram their only son?"

"No, sir."

"Oh, he has siblings?"

"No, sir."

"Go on! Don't make me dig information out of you." Pisacha's eyes gleamed. "However, if you prefer it, I can arrange to do just that."

"It is a bit of a mystery, sire. Apparently, Kuyavan is not Vikram's father. This was one of the things the astrologer told Vikram before he and his friends undertook the expedition out of Orum, sire."

"Just call me boss. Don't call me sire. I am not your father. Wait... this gives me an idea."

Dussakuni and Abhishtu waited for Pisacha to continue. Pisacha, however, was silent. He was deep in thought.

"Boss, you were talking about an idea," said Abhishtu.

"Never mind. Don't change the topic. Where are they now?"

"As I said, boss—"

"—We don't know. There is very little chance they will survive all the tests. Let us, however, be prepared for the eventuality. Make sure that the only exit from the maze leads into Rakta Katteri's temple. If required, I will meet them there and haha, reason with them."

"Yes, boss."

"More wine, Trijada!"

CHAPTER FORTY-THREE

THE MAZE

Blood trickled down Bija's neck even as Vikram watched with a feeling of helplessness. A drop of it was surely going to fall on the ground very soon. Vikram turned his face away.

Then he saw something incredible. What started out as a multicolored streak turned into a black swath that moved toward the fallen Bija's neck. A vampire bat lapped up the last drop of blood. It was all over in an instant. Bramara transformed back into a parrot.

"Grin, grin," he said.

"What..." Vikram hadn't fully recovered from the shock of seeing Bramara feed on Bija's blood. He also felt a little groggy from the loss of his own.

"You know parrots can't display facial expressions. I use words instead. Ugh," he added.

"Great that you had the presence of mind to do it without letting the blood drip to the ground," said Dwipada.

"I guess I did okay. But you know there is good blood and bad blood. Bad blood tastes awful. Hey, I bet you can't say this real fast three times, 'Good blood, bad blood'."

"You must be a little dazed from the blood you drank. Why don't you rest a bit?" Ponni offered her arm.

"You can nurse him later," said an irate Dwipada. "Time to leave."

They exited the courtyard through the opening from which the Rakta Bija had emerged. They found themselves in front of a squat building. Almost immediately, Ponni spotted a signboard. *"Figure out the maze,"* read the sign.

"I can figure it out." Vikram took a few steps to the entrance of the building and stumbled. He would have fallen but for Ponni who caught him.

"His wound needs attending to," Jabala rummaged in her shoulder bag and brought out a vial and bandages.

"Ow, that hurts."

"I haven't even started cleaning the wound." Jabala sprinkled the contents of the vial on a bandage that she wound firmly around his shoulder.

"Let me go now," said Vikram.

"You can't. You need to rest the shoulder for a couple of hours."

"But I have to solve the maze. Bramara can fly over it and give me its layout. I can then draw it out on the ground and find the shortest way out."

"That won't work," said Bramara, "I just checked. You can't get an aerial view. This maze is in a building that's closed on top."

No one spoke. Vikram broke the silence. "I once thought of a method to solve any maze. I am sure it will work."

"Vikram and Dwipada are in no condition to wander inside a maze for hours," said Jabala. "Someone else should go ahead. Once a way has been figured out, the others can follow."

"I can go," said Madavi, "if you tell me what to do."

"I will go with you," said Kalla. "We will return to take you through the maze."

"You will need something to mark the walls," said Vikram.

"That's no problem. We have a heap of soft white stones here. Those markings will easily show up on the walls."

"This is what you have to do," said Vikram, "You mark a line on the wall wherever you go. If you reach a blind end, retrace your steps and continue to mark. If you reach a junction that you haven't been to before..."

"How will I know whether I have visited a junction before?"

"Wait…" Vikram held up a hand. He was now breathing heavily. He paused a little and continued. "If you have already visited a junction, you will have a marking on at least one of the paths branching from there. That's how you will know that you have visited a junction."

"If you haven't been to the junction, choose any of the branches at random and walk along that passage. If you see a branching point you have been to before and you are walking along a once-marked path, retrace your path and go back to the previous junction. If you are walking along a twice-marked path when you reach the junction, take a path you haven't been on before. If none is available, take one that is marked once.

"Eventually, you will reach the exit. The most direct path is the one marked exactly once."

"I am impressed," said Madavi. "What happens if there is no exit at all?"

Then I must bid goodbye to both of you. He thought for a while and said, "Unfortunately, no. You will return to the entrance with all paths marked twice."

"I am sorry," said Kalla, "I am a little lost."

"Already?" said Vikram.

"So am I," admitted Madavi. "I asked you the question only because it seemed like an intelligent question to ask."

"I have thought up a little verse to help you remember the rules. Why don't you write it down?" Bana fished out a palm-leaf and a scriber from his pocket. Madavi wrote it down as Vikram recited—

"At a dead-end, whence you came, return.

So with a new path and an old turn.

With a new path and a new junction,

Take any new path with no distinction.

While a once-trodden path traversing,

On a junction beholding,

Tread any new path if one does show,

Else, a once-marked path follow."

Kalla read it aloud thrice. "Now it's clear."

"Not bad," Bana said, "though it doesn't quite rhyme. I think 'compunction' would have been better than 'distinction'. And in which world does 'traversing' rhyme with 'beholding'? 'Perusing' would have been better. I am not saying it would have been ideal. But certainly better."

"Critics!" Vikram rolled his eyes.

"Wish us luck," said Madavi, as they prepared to enter the maze.

Kalla marked the walls while Madavi led the way. The inside of the maze was surprisingly bright with light coming in from semi-transparent slabs embedded in the ceiling.

They followed the rules Vikram had laid out and must have walked for an hour or so, wildly choosing turns whenever they came to a junction.

Madavi kept turning around to see if Kalla was following.

"You hardly make any sound while walking," exclaimed Madavi, still looking at him. Kalla smiled.

"Watch where you are going..."

Kalla saw Madavi stumble. His reflexes kicked in. In a moment, he pulled her back. It took Madavi a while to recover her poise.

"Who would have expected a trap door right in the middle of the path?"

"Do you know what it means?" asked Kalla.

"Yes," Madavi said with a faint smile. "I am safe when you are around."

"That's not what I meant," said Kalla. "This is not a trap door. It's a passage. We are in a godforsaken three-dimensional maze."

"I hope the method that Vikram figured out works with three-dimensional mazes," said Kalla. "We have no choice anyway. We'll continue using the same method."

Steps led down from the opening that tripped Madavi up.

They decided to go down. They had hardly gone down twenty steps when—

"Is it my imagination or is it getting really dark around here?" asked Madavi. She sounded worried.

"We are underground now and there is no source of light. But don't worry," reasoned Kalla.

"But how will we—"

"—see the markings on the wall? Look behind here," Kalla pointed to the wall.

The marks Kalla made glowed green in the dark.

"I used a special fluorescent marker—part of a kit that I carry. We use it in the trade to signal each other." Kalla preened a little.

The maze seemed unending, continually twisting and turning. They had been walking for nearly three hours.

"Vikram's method does not talk about holding hands," Madavi said.

"But this really helps. This will mean that we won't get lost in the dark."

"You mean, if we do get lost, we will be lost together," said Madavi. Suddenly, Madavi's grip tightened around Kalla's hand.

"Something heavy just ran over my feet," she whispered.

In the dim light, Kalla saw it—the largest rat he had ever seen.

"Let's follow it," shouted Kalla as he ran behind the rat. Soon they came to a point where the path split into four. The rat took the path that sloped upwards. Kalla followed it, dragging the marker across the wall even as he ran. It was getting brighter all the while.

They turned a corner and halted in relief. Four columns supported a large roof overhead. Light was streaming through an opening in the wall.

"At last," said Kalla.

"How did you decide to follow the rat? That probably saved us a couple of hours.

"Well," said Kalla trying to look modest. "I have heard rats can be trained to negotiate mazes. I thought this one must be—"

"Shhh!" said Madavi, with fingers on her lips.

They heard heavy footsteps. Madavi quickly pulled Kalla behind one of the columns. Kalla let go of Madavi's hand. He held his left wrist with his right hand as Madavi stared, puzzled.

They remained behind the column till the steps faded. "We can go and fetch the others," said Kalla. They hurried on their way back.

"STOP THAT!" shouted Madavi as she saw Kalla trying to mark the way again. Kalla froze.

"We are supposed to follow the singly-marked path. If you mark these again, we will be in trouble."

"Sorry, forgot. Force of habit, I guess."

"What was that bit about holding your wrists back there? Are you hurt or something?"

"No. I was just timing the sentries with my pulse. It took them 140 beats to return from one end. From the other end it took them 400 beats. This will be useful when we return."

It took them just under half an hour to get back to the entrance.

Vikram had rested and was feeling better. The concern that Ponni showed contributed more than a little to his sense of well-being.

"I didn't realize it could be a three-dimensional maze," he told Kalla. "I am not sure if my algorithm works in three dimensions. Anyway, the great thing is—it worked and you are here."

"This should be the last obstacle. After this, we are likely to come face-to-face with Pisacha."

They walked through the maze, following the once-marked path till they reached the place where Kalla and Madavi had seen the sentries.

CHAPTER FORTY-FOUR

THE CASTLE

Vikram was in a hurry to step outside the maze. Kalla bade them wait till the sentries crossed over to the longer beat.

As they came out of the maze, it took some time for their eyes adjust to natural light. Vikram had to squint a little to see properly. They were in a courtyard. Just ahead of them was a door that was shut with a crossbar and locked. There was another doorway on the side, from which came a continuous grinding noise.

"Let me check. There are very few locks that I cannot open in two seconds," said Kalla, as he stepped forward. "Maybe I can see more clearly if you move a little," he told Madavi who was standing in front of him.

"Sorry," said Madavi as she stepped away.

He inspected the lock on the door. "Unfortunately for us, this lock is one of those created by Viswakarma."

Vikram ran towards the other doorway, Bramara teetering on his shoulder. Kalla and Madavi remained at the barred door while the others joined Vikram.

Two statues stood on either side of the opening. Vikram studied them keenly. He took in the sharp incisors, the backward pointing feet, the horns on their heads and the instruments of torture placed in their hands. *Asura demons.*

"This must be an entrance to a temple. These statues are of its guards." Dwipada said.

A metal cylinder spun slowly in the middle of the doorway. It was as tall as the doorway and occupied half its width. As the surface of the cylinder emerged from the right, it revealed sharp blades that nearly touched the sides of the doorway. As it rotated further, the blades retracted and were replaced by blunt shafts.

They stood there, mesmerized by the shafts going in and the blades emerging. Bana observed it carefully for a while before he spoke.

"Stupid design. They could have avoided all of this. Could just have had fixed blades jutting out from the right side."

"But what is it?" Asadu asked.

"It is a one-way door," said Dwipada. "You can go in, but cannot come out. At least not come out whole."

He had hardly finished saying this when Vikram rushed in through the revolving door.

"A pity we can't enter then," said Madavi.

"I didn't say I couldn't open it. Not that any of my fellow members could have opened it. If I had a metallic strip or something…"

Madavi pulled out a hairpin from her hair.

"Will this do?"

Kalla took the proffered pin. His brows knit in concentration.

"Do you mind turning away for a moment?" Kalla asked after he had been at work for a minute or two. "A watched lock doesn't open."

Madavi looked away. A click and the lock sprang open. She looked back in surprise.

"I could have kissed you now," she said.

"Show, don't tell," said Kalla, as he puckered up.

"We don't have time for this. Let's call the others."

Kalla turned around to see Vikram disappear into the other doorway, followed by the others.

"Wait!" Kalla shouted.

Kalla and Madavi ran after them. When they reached the doorway, they found their entry barred by a now stationary cylinder with knives jutting out from its surface.

Kalla was the first to recover. "We have no choice—let's go through the door I just unlocked. Maybe both these are entrances to the temple. Or it might lead to Pisacha's quarters."

"Let's go," she said.

Madavi and Kalla ran back and entered through the unlocked door.

"Let's bolt it behind us," said Madavi. "This will prevent guards from coming in after us."

"Great idea," said Kalla." We should look for other entrances as well and lock them."

There was very little light inside once they had closed the door. They stumbled down a set of narrow steps.

Vikram found himself in a large rectangular hall with a high ceiling. On either side, stone pillars with intricately carved shafts extended to the roof. Scenes from the twenty-eight subsidiary hells were depicted in graphic detail on one of its walls. The capital of each pillar was decorated with stone onions, with their tips pointing downwards. Bats hung upside down. The base of every pillar resembled a vat for boiling oil, used in hell to dip inmates as punishment. Demons, bats and snakes leered from every corner.

Vikram's mind was a cauldron of seething emotions. He thought of his father, the gentle Kuyavan, and his feisty mother, Durga. *Do I really want to know the secret of my birth? The astrologer said something about it. Both Bramara and Dwipada indicated that I would find the mystery behind my birth here.* He thought of Aditya. He thought of his friends and of Ponni. Suddenly, he remembered the box he had brought with him that was tied to his upper cloth.

While Vikram stood lost in thought, Ponni joined him. It suddenly grew still. Vikram and Ponni looked at each other. "It's the cylinder," said Asadu. "It has stopped rotating."

"Madavi!" cried Ponni.

"I am afraid she and Kalla have been left behind," said Asadu.

They looked at each other. Finally, Vikram spoke. "Kalla is resourceful, I am sure they will manage. We must move on."

I hope they do. I hope they are safe.

The ground was paved with crude black stones. The atmosphere of gloom affected their moods. They moved inwards along a radial path in silence. The only sounds inside were from the bats that wheeled around, flapping their wings. The group pushed aside thick cobwebs as they pressed forward. The passage from the pillared hall led them to a room with a low ceiling. The light was dim. What they saw in there made them shudder in horror.

"Sire...boss, it looks like they have crossed the maze successfully. Shall I order the soldiers to capture them?" Abhishtu was breathless as he came running into Pisacha's chamber.

"Fool, if I wanted to use the soldiers, I would have done so earlier. I want the boy alive and willing. He has the signs of the conch and the wheel on his palm. I have to sacrifice him to Rakta Katteri. I would prefer he comes to me on his own volition.

"Trijada," he called out. There was no response. "TRIJADA!" he shouted.

"She is, er... standing right there and nodding her head, boss," said Abhishtu, indicating her position with his eyes.

"Abhishtu, never ever communicate with your eyes. The next time you do so will be your last time. Trijada, go to the cellar and bring me a pitcher of the best vintage I have. I am leaving now. If I haven't returned by the time you are back, leave it on the table. You know my best wine, don't you?"

"It's in a cask with a silver stopper, marked with a skull and crossbones. I shall soon have reason to celebrate."

As Trijada left, Pisacha turned to Abhishtu.

"In any case, have a hundred soldiers ready for action," he ordered. "Let them gather at the northern entrance, ready to enter the temple on a signal from us. Send a dozen of them to guard it. Give them orders to not injure the boy in any way. Let them concentrate on the bearded one. Come with me. We will go and meet the interlopers."

He halted in front of a mirror in the room to admire himself.

"What's that?" Ponni gasped.

In the room they saw a metal chair on a platform with straps and chains placed beside it. Its seat was an iron grill. Below the chair was a sharp spearhead with a base as thick as a man's wrist. A lever mechanism could raise or lower it. There were black stains on the ground just below the chair.

"That's a machine for impaling," replied Asadu.

Vikram felt a kind of anger he had never known before.

On the left were rows of benches filled with various instruments of torture. There were spiked chains, branding irons, hooks, pincers, forceps, tongs, pliers, rusty nails, hammers and blades of different kinds.

Boilers, cauldrons and kegs of oils sat in a corner.

"I wonder what this is used for," said Asadu, picking up a pair of oddly-shaped forceps.

"You do not want to know," said Dwipada.

Propped on a bench was a skeleton with only the skull and the leg bones showing. The rest was wrapped tightly in animal skin.

"Must have been a really thin person," said Asadu.

"Not really," said Dwipada. When you wrap the hide of a freshly flayed animal around someone, it tightens as it dries, crushing the ribs and internal organs."

When they came across a lime pit with bits of clothing floating about, no one spoke. They just hurried past, averting their eyes. Vikram was not sure whether the stench of blood and rotting bodies was real or imagined.

Walking ahead, they came to a broad flight of steps ascending to a platform. There were only about twenty of them but they were steep. Vikram and Ponni took the steps two at a time. They reached the top ahead of the others. A closed wooden door, black with age, greeted them. As they halted, the door flew open and armed guards spilled out.

Kalla and Madavi raced down the steps. By the time they managed to break the momentum and slow down, the steps ended abruptly. Light from a torch on a bracket shone on a cobblestone passage. The ceiling was low and was supported with rafters painted black.

Madavi pulled out the torch from the bracket.

"You walk in front," said Kalla. "Otherwise my shadow can be seen by someone ahead."

They turned a corner, almost running into two guards. The spears the men held were at least two heads taller than them. They wore black tunics and leggings with a stripe of red running right across the length.

"Who is there?" called out one of the guards.

"You mean," corrected the other, "HALT, who goes there?"

Madavi recovered from the shock quickly, held the torch higher and took a quick look behind. Kalla was not to be seen.

The guards had their spears pointed at Madavi.

"Take it easy folks," said Madavi, forcing a smile. "I am a friend."

Where is Kalla?

"Hah, don't try to trick us because—"

He couldn't finish what he wanted to say. Kalla, who had been hanging from a rafter, dropped on him. Before the other man could react, Kalla struck him hard in the neck with his hand, fingers extended. Both the guards were now on the ground, writhing in pain. Kalla held them pinned. Madavi bent down with her dagger in hand and soon, thin lines of blood appeared on the cheeks of the soldiers.

"Madavi, what are you doing?"

"Don't worry. The tip of my dagger is coated with a sedative that will ensure they sleep for at least a couple of hours."

"When they get up, they will feel very sick and throw up repeatedly for some time," continued Madavi.

"Just don't wave the dagger about," said Kalla.

The narrow path was winding. They walked along for what seemed a very long time till they reached a large room.

The room was empty. In the middle was a raised platform covered with a rug made of animal skins stitched together. Right in front of the platform stood a hollow pentagon-shaped structure made of bricks. A garland of human skulls hung on a nail from a wall. A spherical crystal glowed atop an obsidian table.

Kalla knew instantly that this was Pisacha Pinda's chamber. As they moved to the middle of the room, Madavi froze on hearing the footsteps of someone running behind another door.

CHAPTER FORTY-FIVE

AT THE CHAMBER

Vikram and Ponni heard shouts of 'Victory to Pisacha Pinda' from the guards even before they saw them.

The guards wore black tunics and divided skirts. Some of them held aloft huge curved swords serrated on one edge. When they saw Ponni and Vikram, three guards rushed at Ponni while the others encircled them. Ponni reacted quickly. She thrust her dagger straight into the tunic of the first soldier. When she pulled it out, pushing at the guard with her free hand, it came out red and the guard collapsed. Vikram saw that they were trying to isolate Ponni and attack her while trying to capture him alive.

"Back to back," he shouted to Ponni. There was an urgency in his voice. Ponni moved away from the attackers and joined Vikram. They stood with their backs to each other as a single fighting unit, Vikram ahead of Ponni.

One of the opponents was large and muscular. He attacked with a speed and frenzied vigor that Vikram would not have thought possible in such a large man. Vikram had to parry repeatedly to thwart the attack. Soon it was clear that the man was trying to get at Ponni and was not intent on killing Vikram. The man feinted and tried to get past Vikram. Vikram saw an opening in the form of an exposed neck and thrust at it decisively. The guard fell, bleeding profusely from a ripped jugular vein. In the meantime, another guard slipped past Vikram and engaged with Ponni at close quarters.

By then, the rest of the group reached the top of the platform. Asadu saw Ponni being attacked. He drew his bow and soon, an arrow was sticking out of the soldier's back. The soldier fell heavily to the ground.

"That was unnecessary," said Ponni, as she flashed a brief smile at Asadu. She turned the fallen opponent over with her foot and pointed her dagger at the bloody cut in his abdomen.

She hardly finished saying this when three more joined the fray. The new entrants were obviously veterans. Even though they were armed with spears, they kept their distance and tried to distract the couple.

Dwipada was not having it easy. Three guards surrounded him. Dwipada whirled his ax around to hold them at bay. Jabala stood next to him, apparently unarmed, with a look of helplessness on her face. One of the guards attacking Dwipada noted this and rushed at her with a raised sword and with obvious glee. The expression on Jabala's face hardly changed as her foot connected with his body. The soldier's neck whiplashed and he fell.

Two others rushed at Jabala, one raising his sword high above with the intention of bringing it down on her head, when Bana intervened. He stabbed him with his scriber, saying, "Die, you villainous cur," his voice quivering with disdain. The other got close to her, trying to envelop her in a bear hug. Jabala kicked him in the face to see him fall, flailing.

A huge guard engaged Asadu. He shouldered his bow and wielded his *silambu* instead. The stick twirled around and when it descended, it came crashing down on the soldier's head.

Dwipada was tired. Vikram wanted to help him but was kept busy by some of the soldiers. Dwipada swung his ax wildly and two of his attackers fell clutching at their throats. The floor was slick with blood. To his horror, Vikram saw Dwipada too was bleeding from a deep gash on his side. Jabala and Asadu noticed it as well. Asadu quickly disposed off the second of the two attackers. They rushed to Dwipada's defense but not before Dwipada fell, taking the last soldier down with him. He was bleeding profusely from his wound.

CHAPTER FORTY-SIX

AT THE TEMPLE

Vikram reversed his sword and knocked his opponent down with its pommel. By then, Ponni had moved away from her opponent. She shot an arrow through him. Vikram wiped the blood off his face with the clothes of a slain soldier. To his relief, he found that most of the blood was not his, though there was some bleeding from a cut below his cheeks. His arms and legs ached from multiple cuts and bruises as he rushed towards Dwipada.

Jabala tore a long strip of cloth from the a border of her sari and tied it around Dwipada's upper arm. She took a small wooden rod from the bag she carried, inserted it into the knot and twisted it till she was satisfied.

"Hold on to this stick. The pressure must be maintained," she told Asadu who took hold of the stick from her.

"Is he badly injured?" Vikram was breathless.

Dwipada opened his eyes. "Don't worry, Vikram," he said, "I will be fine. I am really tough." He stopped. Even to speak was an effort.

"*Guru* Dwipada...," Vikram started to say something but his voice trailed off.

Dwipada's eyes opened a little wider. It was easy to imagine his lips curved up in a weak smile behind his beard. "My blessings are with you, Vikram, even if I may not be with you when you confront Pisacha."

"That's exactly it, *apeechiko*. We have come so far because of Ponni, Kalla, Bana and others. I have done very little to contribute. I am not even sure I am capable of..."

"You don't know your own strength, Vikram. Even the great Hanuman had to be reminded of what he was capable of before he could cross the ocean." Dwipada paused to recover his breath. "In the fight to come, you will have to fight alone. I can assure you that you will find the strength from within. My blessings to you." Dwipada closed his eyes.

Jabala looked up and smiled reassuringly, seeing the concern on Vikram's face.

"I have stopped the loss of blood. Within half an hour, he should be feeling much better. But the next half hour is critical. I will then apply a poultice and he should then be ready for further battles if necessary. I suggest the three of you and Bramara go ahead. Asadu and I will wait here."

Bana reached for the scriber and palm leaves at his waist and scribbled hard.

"My mother can handle this," said Ponni as she rushed toward the black door. "There are bound to be hundreds of soldiers around. We need to get the Chintamani before they are alerted."

They had to run with care as the floor was slippery with blood. An eerie silence reigned as they made their way through the door. Ponni quietly slipped her hand in Vikram's. They now had the first view of the dread form of Rakta Katteri.

Kalla reacted quickly. He rushed out the door, following the sound of the footsteps. He merged with the shadows. He noted that the runner was physically unfit. As the person approached him, he heard his panting and wheezing louder than his footfalls. Kalla stuck a foot out and the runner went sprawling. The man didn't attempt to get up for a while and sat dazed on uneven cobblestones. Kalla quickly tied a piece of cloth around his neck when Madavi broke the silence.

"From the way he is dressed, he looks like a minister or somebody close to Pisacha." The man on the floor looked around with a blank stare.

"You will of course tell Mother everything, won't you?" Madavi's voice took on a mellifluous monotone and the man's eyes were riveted on her.

"You will answer the lady." Kalla tightened the cloth around his neck just a little.

"Who...who...are you? If Pisacha finds out, you are dead meat."

Kalla's twisted the cloth a little more.

"Okay, okay...d...don't hurt me. I'll tell you whatever you want to know." The man's hands flailed uselessly at his throat.

"That's better," said Madavi. "We will ask all the questions. To begin with, what's your name? What are you to Pisacha?"

Kalla loosened the cloth a little to allow him to speak.

"I am Abhishtu, Pisacha's chief minister. If you let me go, I can intercede for you with Pisacha..."

"Shut up and answer the question. Why were you running?"

"We have intruders at the temple and Pisacha asked me to fetch the guards."

Kalla held up his hand, asking Madavi to be quiet. With the other hand, he gave the twisted cloth a shake.

"Now tell me—where is the main body of guards stationed?"

"Don't be rough. They are at the end of this passageway." Abhishtu indicated the direction in which he was headed. "Once I call them, they will come into the temple. In any case, I have instructed them to wait for a while and rush in."

"So that's what you were going to do. You wanted to alert the soldiers?"

"All right. Get me that rope!" Kalla instructed Madavi, pointing at a tangle that lay on a chair.

"That's no rope," said Abhishtu. "That's Pisacha's belt."

"That reminds me..." said Kalla. He took Pisacha's silk robe from the chair and stuffed it into Abhishtu's mouth.

He then tied his hands and feet expertly with Pisacha's belt, dumping him to one side.

"Let's leave this place quickly," said Kalla turning to Madavi, "We need to lock the other entrance to the temple."

The guards were about to enter the temple as Kalla and Madavi reached the massive iron door. It took a huge effort but they were able to close and lock it before the guards could come in.

Madavi was breathing hard but Kalla simply turned around and started running. They went past the turn-off to Pisacha's room.

They were a few steps away from the temple's inner door when they heard an explosion that was louder than any Kalla had heard before.

CHAPTER FORTY-SEVEN

RAKTA KATTERI

Vikram and Ponni stood at the threshold of the inner sanctum of the temple.

Rakta Katteri was an imposing figure of black stone, oiled all over, shiny with dark malevolence. She was seated on a saber-toothed tiger, holding a decapitated human head in one hand and a pot stained dark red in another. Her many arms bore different weapons—a short curved sword, a lasso, a disc with serrated edges, an iron mace and a trident. Her sharp canines dripped blood. Her emerald green eyes glittered in the light of the single lamp that hung from the rafters, forming weird shadows that undulated on the floor. She wore a skirt of dismembered limbs.

In front of her was the sacrificial altar—a large black granite monolith, flat on top with a thick encrustation of a dark material.

Vikram's mind filled with fear. He gripped Ponni's hand as his other hand tightened on his sword. Bramara was in a strange mood. He fluffed out his feathers and inched closer to Vikram's face.

"The Chintamani!" Bramara shrieked suddenly, jerking Vikram's hands, causing him to let go off Ponni. Bramara flew off his shoulders.

The Chintamani coruscated from a gold chain that hung around Rakta Katteri's neck. Vikram took a step towards the idol. He froze as three figures appeared from behind the statue.

He immediately identified Pisacha, a head taller than the others. The spy stood next to him.

"The other one must be Abhishtu," Ponni whispered.

As Pisacha's companions lit a few torches on the wall behind Katteri, his form came into full view. He was in the formal dress of a high mage—tiger skin wrapped around his waist and slung over a shoulder, hands and arms painted with arcane symbols in red, eyes blackened with kohl, a large vermilion streak on his forehead and a garland of guffawing skulls whose mandibles were attached to the cranium. He held in one hand a carved ebony wand that glowed green. A thin long scabbard was strapped to his waist. He grinned suddenly as his hand moved to point the ebony stick at Vikram.

"Quick, Vikram, FIRE!" screeched Bramara, who had now taken to air.

Ponni reached for her quiver. The sorcerer's wand followed Bramara, who was now on Bana's shoulders. The jewel on Katteri's neck brightened. There was a rush of air over Vikram's head and toward Bramara and Bana. A semi-transparent cage formed around them. It lifted and hung in mid-air with Bramara flapping his wings furiously and screeching. Bana had his scriber out. Vikram turned his attention back to Pisacha. Tension burned in him. Ponni pulled back the bow string and let go an arrow. The rod in Pisacha's hand turned in her direction. A soundless blackness issued from it, crashing into her. The impact threw Ponni back and down on to the floor and she lay motionless. Ponni's arrow buried itself in Pisacha's shoulder. The wind caused by the passing blackness rocked Vikram sideways, though his concentration did not waver.

Pisacha screamed in agony as he tore the arrow from his shoulder.

"EARTH, FIRE!" shouted Vikram as he cast a spell to form a fireball as large as a man's head that sped towards Pisacha. He drew his sword and rushed at Pisacha.

Pisacha ducked under the fireball. It hit Dussakuni who was hiding behind him. Dussakuni fell, face blackened and beard charred. Pisacha tucked the ebony rod into his waistband. He placed his hand on the pommel of his sword. His other arm hung limply from his shoulder.

Pisacha's sword hissed out of the scabbard. Bands of light streaked down the length of the weapon. Their swords met with a high-pitched screech of fingernails on a hard surface. Vikram felt a massive shock that originated from the tips of his fingers and radiated to his shoulders. He grimaced in pain. Pisacha was waving his sword with ridiculous ease as though he was using a feather duster. All of a sudden, his sword darted, entered Vikram's side. The smoky sword had a pink tip.

Vikram tried to blink away the intense pain. He pressed one hand to his side and fought on. Every time the swords clashed, his pain increased. He was tiring now. His mind went back to the *silambu* fight he had with his master. Now or never. His sword was drawn back for a fierce thrust even as the opponent's sword went back and streaked towards his chest. Instead of an immediate counter, Vikram's attack segued into a parry, knocking aside the attack, and a parry turned into a thrust.

It was a perfect feint and attack. Or so he thought.

The sword should have pierced through sinew and bone in the sorcerer's chest. Instead it met a steel plate. The sword shattered into fragments, sounding like an avalanche of steel.

Vikram stepped several paces back in astonishment, his hand holding the broken stump of the weapon. Pisacha didn't bother to pursue him immediately. His laughter mingled with the experimental swishes he made in the air.

"Abhishtu, call the guards," Pisacha shouted. Abhishtu emerged from behind the image and scurried out of sight.

Vikram saw Ponni lying unconscious and Bramara trapped in a cage. He thought of Dwipada lying in a pool of blood. He thought of Aditya. It is up to me now. He emptied his mind of thought as he gestured at the large stone altar and shouted "LIFT!"

The huge stone altar creaked and heaved. It soon came away, completely free from its moorings and rose up in the air.

Cockroaches, scorpions, queerly-shaped bugs that had taken shelter under the stone scurried out of the glistening wet space underneath. The stone rose rapidly, almost to the high ceiling, and at a gesture from Vikram, started to come down on Pisacha.

Pisacha now came to life. He pulled out the rod from his waist with difficulty using his injured hand. The red jewel on Rakta Katteri's neck began pulsating. The altar hung motionless just a few feet above his head. Lines of fracture appeared on its surface and deepened rapidly. Then it burst with a loud noise. One of the larger fragments crashed on top of Pisacha's legs and pinned him to the floor. His face was bloodied. One of his eyes, where a large chunk of a stone hit him, was closed and swollen. He still held on to his wand. It no longer had its green luster.

Vikram closed his eyes. Pieces of stone buffeted him. He opened his eyes and wiped his bloodied face. He shook his head to clear it.

"You are proving to be worthy of me." The words from Pisacha's lips were slow and deliberate. His metallic voice was oddly comforting.

"Huh!" cried Vikram as Pisacha's one eye bored into him. The rod in Pisacha's hand pulsed green. For a moment, Vikram was distracted by the jewel in Rakta Katteri's neck that pulsed in step. Pisacha's soothing voice drew him back. Vikram's mind grew cloudy. Once on a dare, Vikram had jumped into a muddy lake. He felt now as he had then, swimming through murky waters.

"Vikram, my son, come to me. Join me. Together we can rule the world."

"What...what do you mean?"

Pisacha grimaced in pain and took a long breath. The wand now pulsed brighter.

"You have the markings on your hands. You could be truly great but you have a lot to learn. I am the best person to teach you. Sit by my side and we can rule the world."

"I am not...interested in ruling the world. I just want—"

"—Aditya and others to be rid of blindness," continued Pisacha.

"I will make that happen. You just have to do what it takes. I know for sure that you have it in you."

"How?" Vikram's mind wandered as Pisacha's eye bored deeper.

"I know for sure because you are my son."

Vikram noticed in an abstracted way that the rod in Pisacha's hand was beginning to glow fiercely. He heard the words as though in a fugue.

"Yes," Pisacha continued, "I met your mother Durga when I was in Akkam on some business. The relationship matured to something stronger. Your mother and I were soon deeply in love. A great woman."

"Yes, isn't she? Why do you keep looking at that stick?" asked Vikram dreamily.

"Never mind. Durga's parents didn't like the idea of us getting married. We decided to run away. They got wind of it and forced her into going on a marriage procession to Orum. She was pregnant by then. I never saw her afterwards."

Vikram thought he heard a voice in his head but wasn't sure.

"Are you saying..."

"Yes. I am your father and you are my son, whom I have not seen till today." His hand now inched towards the fallen stick. *Daivagan had said, Kuyavan is not your father.*

"He lies. Take your awareness to your little finger." The voice in Vikram's head grew more insistent. Almost automatically, Vikram found himself concentrating on his little finger. His head began to clear as his awareness grew.

"QUICK, BEFORE HE USES HIS WAND!"

Vikram snapped out of the hypnotic trance. His face was now set hard. He muttered an invocation to Brahma, the deity of the dreaded Brahmastra. He aimed the stump of the sword he was holding at Pisacha, just as the sorcerer managed to bring his wand around.

Vikram released the Brahmastra. A searing bright spark formed at Vikram's hand and moved towards Pisacha. For a moment, Pisacha was outlined against the bright spark. There was an incredible explosion.

Pisacha disintegrated and his body parts burned to ashes. A breeze from nowhere scattered his ashes everywhere.

The stone floor around the altar cracked at several places and shattered.

Vikram watched in warily as the cage that held Bramara and Bana dissolved. An agitated Bramara emerged and alighted on his shoulders.

"Oh wow, oh wow," Bana kept muttering as he continued making notes in his palm-leaf notebook.

"Vikram, what was that sound?" Kalla came running in, with Madavi in tow.

"Looks like you have things under control," Dwipada's voice reached him before he came in, supported by Jabala and Asadu.

Ponni ran to her mother and they embraced.

"I see you have taken care of almost everything," said Asadu as he walked up to the idol of Rakta Katteri and removed the jewel from her neck. It no longer pulsated. He took off his silk upper cloth, wrapped the jewel reverently in it and gave it to Dwipada. For the first time, Dwipada's beard parted and chin dimpled when he smiled.

"I have other treasures to pursue," said Asadu and walked rapidly towards the door through which Pisacha had come.

Vikram could only stare. He looked at Bana and thought of Aditya and Orum.

CHAPTER FORTY-EIGHT

ASADU

Asadu hurried along the path that Pisacha had taken earlier and found himself in a chamber. He saw a table with a cracked crystal on top and a chair made of human bones. He also noticed a garland of skulls. *This must be Pisacha's chamber. The treasure should be around here.*

He rummaged through the room. He discovered a cupboard full of maimed dolls. In another, there were feathers of every description. Yet another had vials of different colored liquids, powders and granules.

He stood in the middle of the room. *It must be around somewhere here.*

A movement behind alerted him. He turned around. He was stunned by the vision that appeared in front of him. A well-proportioned woman stood in front of him. Her head was bowed. *Such modesty! Her complexion—fair to the extent of being almost white!* His heart nearly stopped. Two braids hung over her bosom. She had large kohl-lined eyes.

She peeped through her eyelashes.

Asadu realized that anyone can, with a bit of practice, peer through their eyelashes. If you are naturally shortsighted, it helps. Peeping—that took a queen of a woman to perform.

As Asadu stood staring, the vision came nearer. She had a pitcher and a mug in her hands. This was Asadu's dream come true. *If only she had a bunch of grapes as well...*

"The grapes are on the table," Trijada said.

The melody in her voice jerked Asadu back to reality. *This is an opportunity of a lifetime. I cannot let this go. I cannot be tongue-tied.*

Trijada held out the mug. "I am Trijada. Who are you? Where is Pisacha?" she asked.

This woke the silver-tongued orator in Asadu.

"Pisacha? Who cares a fig about Pisacha? The two-*kasu* magician is history. I am the greatest magician known to earth-kind. Behold Asadu!"

He struck a heroic pose and continued.

"When I say '*Choo mandrakkali*'..."

He noticed the sudden glazing over of the eyes and the subtle stiffening of the body that came over Trijada.

"...People prostrate in front of me. They..."

Asadu was shocked to see Trijada fall down and prostrate herself. He was pleased but decided to act embarrassed.

"Hey, don't take it literally. Come, come now. Don't kowtow before me. You are the one who should be treasured and..." Even as he helped her up, he realized that he had been somewhat sidetracked.

"Trijada, you seem to be such a helpful girl. Would you know where Pisacha keeps his treasure?"

"Of course," said Trijada. "I will lead you to it."

CHAPTER FORTY-NINE

A MYSTERY SOLVED

"Ponni, I need to speak to you," said Vikram, taking hold of her hand and guiding her behind a pillar.

Ponni's face showed a mixture of surprise and happiness. "Of course, Vikram," she said with a touch of coyness. "Anything for you."

"I want to speak to you."

"I am ready," said Ponni, a smile playing on her lips.

"I…"

"Go on, Vikram."

"It's nothing important," said Vikram and hurried away. Ponni stared at his retreating form.

"You're an idiot," said Kalla when he found Vikram moping. "A dumb idiot. Speak to her and tell her you love her."

"I need to talk to you," said Vikram, when he found Ponni alone again.

"I need to talk to you." Bramara alighted on Vikram's shoulder.

"Hey," said Ponni. "If you guys need to speak in private, go ahead. I'll leave." Vikram found it difficult to look daggers at Bramara, who was on his shoulder.

"Ponni, stay. I don't want to keep secrets from you." Ponni smiled. Bramara continued. "I have something to tell you. I am not really a parrot."

"I know you are a bee sometimes. You told me all about the birds and bees."

"That's not what I mean, Vikram."

"There is something I want say first, Bramara. You have done more than anyone else for me. You have guided me and you have taught me a lot. You have come to my help whenever I needed it. You have helped me grow. I don't know if I can thank you enough. Of course, I haven't cracked the mystery of my birth. But that's not important. I am fortunate to have people like my parents, and friends like you, who have done so much for me."

"Actually, that's what I wanted to speak to you about. I was a Gandharva. Bramara Sena. Bramara for short."

Seeing Vikram's blank expression, he continued to explain.

"Gandharvas are demi-gods, who are a part of Indra's entourage. In case you don't know who Indra is—he is the king of gods. I was cursed by him to live on earth till I atone for my misdeeds. By helping you, I am now rid of the curse. I am no longer restricted to small forms on earth."

The parrot flew to the ground and in its stead stood a human-looking being, suffused with light.

"Wow," said Vikram, "that was neat! But Bramara, why were you cursed?"

Bramara hung his head in shame. "I was hoping you wouldn't ask. I seduced Durga, your mother. I took the form of a parrot to gain her confidence. I assumed a human form much later in the relationship."

Vikram's expression was unreadable.

"Relationships between humans and gods are forbidden. No wonder Indra cursed you," said Ponni.

"Well," said Bramara with obvious embarrassment, "that was not the problem. You see, we are not allowed to have an unprotected um... relationship with humans. That's why I was cursed."

He then faced Vikram.

"Yes, Vikram, I am your biological father. I could only free myself from the curse by fulfilling the duty of a father towards a son. I was, however, forbidden to reveal the true nature of our relationship until certain conditions were met."

Vikram stared into the distance.

Ponni placed a hand gently on his shoulder. Vikram was quiet for some time before he spoke.

"You understand that this doesn't change anything. I still consider Kuyavan as my father. He has always been there for me. Now, I realize that he has played an even greater role in keeping my family together." He looked up at Bramara.

"I can only think of you as a friend. A great friend."

Vikram's eyes were moist.

"The box," whispered Ponni. "Ask him about the box."

"Oh yes," said Vikram, "I need to ask you something. Do you know what this box is about?" As he spoke, he brought it out.

"Do you know what *diksha* is?" asked Bramara.

"As I know it, it is the transfer of spiritual and other powers from one person to another, typically from *guru* to disciple. It is usually done through touch."

"Very good. You have learned well. *Diksha* can also be imparted through an object. This box, more than anything, contained a father's blessing—my gift to you. Open the box one last time."

Vikram opened the box and found a plain gold ring inside.

"Cool," said Ponni, "that's a magic ring. He just has to rub the ring and you'll appear, right?"

"Well, um... not quite. That ring belongs to Vikram's mother. I just wanted him to return it to her. In fact, the ring I gave her was also in the box once. It was destroyed the last time you opened the box, when you were badly infected by the ghosts of the valley. One last thing before I go. I must tell you that you have made me proud."

"Bramara, I hope you don't mind my calling you that. I now realize that I owe much more to you than I thought. I still think of you as my greatest friend and guide."

"I am happy with that. Whenever you need me in the future, I will come. Will you also tell your mother that I did my duty by you? Now I must go. Wish you all the best."

Even as Bramara flickered and faded, Vikram saw that he winked at him. Vikram thought he detected moisture in Bramara's eyes.

He turned his attention to Ponni.

As they rode back, Vikram noticed the absence of Kalla and Madavi and he remarked on it.

"Just ride a little slower and fall behind a little. I will tell you what they are up to," said Ponni. They hid behind a thick patch of bushes. She told him and showed him.

It was late in the evening when they reached the *ashram*.

Dwipada's wife Aiyo, along with Kamadenu, was waiting for them.

"Aiyo!" exclaimed Dwipada, stretching his hands wide and breaking into a run as he saw her. There was no visible response from Aiyo. Dwipada came to a halt.

"I am sorry," said Dwipada.

Silence.

"I SAID I WAS SORRY," shouted Dwipada.

"I heard you the first time," said Aiyo. "I have been a stone for so long that I have almost lost all ability to feel and react."

"My Aiyo. I will make it up to you for all that. There hasn't been a single day when I haven't rued my hasty actions. Now, I will give you the best of everything. You will realize the full extent of the power of my austerities. I will give you the kind of honeymoon you would have never dreamed of. We will have children. You will have a choice. One truly noble soul or a thousand wastrels. You just have to ask. I hope... your feelings for me haven't changed after my stupid act."

"No, lord of my life. I can assure you that they haven't changed. I have been a chaste and loving wife. I shall continue to be. For instance, should you fall down dead now, I will surely ascend your burning pyre and kill myself. You want to test me, my lord and master? Please go ahead."

"Well... um... that is not so important. I will take your word for it. What is important now is that we have some unfinished work." He turned to Vikram.

"Yes, *apeechiko*, we have a town to save."

"We leave for Orum in four days. We should be there during the full moon."

Dwipada stood at the periphery of the *ashram*. He held the Chintamani in his hand and was turning it around lovingly. At a distance, he could see a horse approaching him. There were two riders; the pillion rider had a cloth covering his face. Soon, he could see the main rider was Asadu.

Asadu got down from the horse at a respectful distance, gestured the pillion rider to stay mounted and approached Dwipada.

"Asadu!" There was joy and a clear welcome in Dwipada's tone. "It is a pleasure to have you back. And I must say you have done a wonderful job. I don't know how you managed to find Pisacha's treasure."

"Your blessings, master," said Asadu.

"You must be tired. Don't worry about your duties today. Rest well. Also, we must be off to Orum tomorrow."

"That is one of the things I want to talk to you about, master."

Dwipada looked questioningly at him. "Go on."

"I won't be coming to Orum with you. I have work to do at Mandala. If we leave things the way they are, Mandala will descend into anarchy."

"So what do you propose to do?"

"I want to make sure Mandala has a new king."

"So, you want to be king, Asadu?

"No master, I will be the chief minister. I want to make Dubaku the king."

"Dubaku... DUBAKU? You mean that idiot of a guard at the gate, who is related to that other idiot, what's his name? Abhishtu?"

"Yes, master. He will, however, be king only in name. He will be an ideal king, because he cannot think for himself, even if you threatened to impale him and fry him in boiling oil. I, as minister, will ensure that things run smoothly. You know, master, I have been a servant for so long that my potential is unexpressed. This will give me an opportunity to—"

"Who's the girl?"

"What do you mean, master? Oh yes, you know the pasts, present and futures. Her name is Trijada. She is the most wonderful person on the earth. She has consented to be my wife."

"Trijada...that rings a bell."

"That was Kamadenu's bell, master."

"I've got it. She was once a physical instructor."

"She told me her whole life story, and she has never been—"

"That was in a previous life. Let me warn you, old habits die hard. That aside, even though I have been inconvenienced, you have my blessings. Have you thought through this idea of making Dubaku a king? Remember, he is related to Abhishtu, who will surely try to control him."

"I have thought about it all, including your being inconvenienced. I must say, in all modesty, you have trained me well." He then turned to the other rider on the horse. "Come here!" he commanded.

The figure approached them. Asadu whipped off the cloth from his face to reveal Abhishtu.

"I thought he is the right person to take my place, master. He is also used to...how shall I put it...respecting authority. Of course, this will mean that Abhishtu will not be able to contribute to rebuilding Mandala."

"Yes—" Abhishtu started to say something.

"—Just consider what your sister will think of you, for having fashioned her son's career so well. You must be prepared to make these little sacrifices. As they say, you cannot make chutney without breaking a coconut."

"Oh my gods, I have been standing here talking while I have a hundred things to do. Farewell, master. Make me proud of you, Abhishtu."

The rider and the horse were soon a speck on the horizon.

CHAPTER FIFTY
CHINTAMANI

Vikram and his companions stood at the gates of Orum. Vikram knew exactly what to do. He grasped the horns of the bull figure on the gates and twisted. His palms burned. The doors dissolved. No sooner had they all hurried through, the gates re-formed.

"I have an idea," said Bana. "Why don't you stand here as a gate-keeper and let people pass through? Isolation of Orum...solved."

"This works only once—once to go out, once to come in," said Dwipada.

"That means we are stuck here forever if we don't free Orum. Why didn't anybody tell me this before?"

"You didn't ask," retorted Dwipada calmly.

"I fervently hope the Chintamani works," said Bana.

Madavi's face suddenly brightened.

"That gives me an idea," she whispered to Kalla. "What if the guild elders were to believe that the Chintamani was stolen by you?"

Kalla thought for a while before he answered. "In that case, they will have to accord me the highest honor. I could get credit for a jewel heist of the century or rather, the millennium."

His face fell as he continued on. "How will they ever believe that?"

Durga and Kuyavan were overjoyed. It was the first time Vikram had seen his father weep. Durga embraced Vikram. Aditya was standing next to them with a broad grin on his face.

"My, how you've grown!" exclaimed Durga. "I guess my adventures have sort of made me leaner and stronger," said Vikram.

"I wasn't talking to you, I was talking to Ponni," said Durga even as she hugged her.

"Cho chweet," continued Durga as she pinched Ponni's cheeks.

Vikram cringed. Ponni giggled.

"Nice voice, I hope she is a looker to match," whispered Aditya.

"She is going to be your sister-in-law. Have some respect," Vikram whispered back.

Vikram gave his parents a short summary of all that had happened.

Dwipada appeared even more serious than usual. He also looked a little nervous.

"While we will use the power of Chintamani to free Orum, we must use the power of the many in doing so."

Dwipada then turned to Vikram. "As I have told you, anything is possible. Things with a low probability of occurrence just need more energy. The energy of the Chintamani can be amplified by the energy of the people concentrating on it. Have as many people as possible gather at the western edge of the town by sunset."

The excitement in the air was palpable. Most of Orum was there to witness the spectacle. Mootha was there, leaning on a stick and keeping a watchful eye over all arrangements. Bautik was present. He held a bundle of palm leaves and a scriber, eager to record the historic moment. Kuyavan was strutting about in self-importance. He kept the crowd from getting too close to Dwipada. Daivagan beamed, revealing his tobacco-stained teeth.

Dwipada looked resplendent. He changed from his bark clothes to an off-white silk cloth with a gold filigree border. He brought out the Chintamani and placed it carefully on a wooden altar, specially constructed per his instructions near the edge of the force field.

He started with an invocation to the elephant-headed god. His voice was majestic as he chanted the mantras. Every now and then he would stop and gesture at the crowd, who would shout 'Aamaan'.

The pitch of his chanting rose. In a dramatic gesture, he brought his hands together and bent to touch Chintamani. The jewel brightened a little, a crackle and pop was heard, and a few wisps of smoke emanated from it. The jewel faded back to its original color. It simply lay there, if anything, duller than before.

CHAPTER FIFTY-ONE

THE SACRIFICE

"The power of the jewel has been discharged completely." Vikram looked at the jewel in disbelief. He shook his head.

Dwipada stared at the jewel for a long time. The crowd became restive. After what seemed an epoch, Dwipada came to a decision.

"Vikram, have them dig a pit about six feet by three feet and about four feet deep."

"*Apeechiko*," said Kuyavan, "you don't have to do it. We have lived this lonely life for ages in Orum and we simply have to continue to do so. It was no fault of yours. Don't dig your own grave. Or rather, don't ask us to."

"I will not be a sage in a rage," Dwipada muttered thrice before he calmed down.

"I do not intend to bury myself. Just get it done."

Vikram, Kalla and Ponni watched the men dig the pit.

"It has taken twice as long as I estimated," said Vikram. "I have seen three men, two women and a child work on a pit five and a half feet by two feet by three feet and complete it in an hour and a half. Now this should have taken only two hours as there are four men."

"Spare me," said Kalla, as he walked away with a pained expression on his face.

"Tell me more," Ponni sidled up to Vikram.

Dwipada changed his clothes again. This time he wore an orange-brown waist-cloth. His face was set. He gestured to the crowd to keep quiet and began his incantations.

As his chanting rose to its final crescendo, he made the Gesture of Consciousness with his left hand and raised his right arm, palm facing down.

A violet light emanated from his right hand. As it struck the pit, it filled with liquid light. Dwipada appeared to get paler and weaker. Vikram thought Dwipada was getting shorter till he realized that he now was standing on the ground. *His feet are touching the ground!*

"Don't do it, *apeechiko!*" Vikram yelled.

It was to no avail. Dwipada continued holding his hand up. At last, the pit was full. Dwipada found it difficult to stay on his feet as he swayed unsteadily. His face was drawn in a grim concentration. The violet light faded away. His hands shook a little as he took the Chintamani from the altar with great care and placed it on the surface of liquid light.

The assembled crowd pushed forward to get a view of the pit. They were astonished by the sight. The jewel had created a spinning vortex on the surface and was rapidly soaking up the violet liquid light. It soon became a glowing ember, lit with fire. Soon the pit was empty of liquid light. Vikram had to shield his eyes to see the incandescent jewel at the bottom of the pit. Dwipada lay to one side of the pit, eyes closed, a ghost of a smile lighting up his face.

'O sage!' Vikram wailed. He rushed to the prone Dwipada.

"You have performed the ultimate sacrifice. You have given up all your yogic powers for the welfare of earth-kind. Master, this is a lesson I will never forget."

"Help me up. I still have things to do," said Dwipada, opening his eyes. "Take the jewel out."

Vikram propped him up and took the jewel from the pit, handling it with utmost veneration.

"Don't give it to me. Throw it with all your strength at the barrier on this side." He indicated a spot to the north where Orum's boundary ended and the invisible force-barrier began.

Vikram picked up a stone and threw it at the force field to determine its position. The stone fell vertically in mid-flight.

He then took the jewel and threw it with all his might at the barrier. Bana instinctively closed his ears and shielded his eyes. Nothing happened for a while. After a few moments, bolts of lightning flashed across the field before they struck the ground. The air around them shimmered. It was several minutes before the display died down.

Scores of people rushed towards what used to be the impenetrable boundary of Orum. There were shouts of joy from those who crossed it. People wanted to carry Dwipada and Vikram on their shoulders in a victory celebration. Vikram politely refused, indicating the sage was too weak and he needed to take care of him.

A wan smile still played across Dwipada's lips. Vikram thought it was tinged with sadness.

CHAPTER FIFTY-TWO

COMEUPPANCE

Asadu sat on a flower-bedecked bed and looked at his wife with pride. He reasoned the time of the 'peace-appointment', when a man starts to know his partner more intimately, was the time to make peace with himself.

"Trijada, my love, I have something to confess."

Trijada stopped pouring a glass of thickened milk into a flowerpot.

"Fair Trijada, I have fooled you. I am not a famous magician. In order to impress you..."

"It is perfectly fine, my-piece-of-crystalline-sugar, I love you for what you are."

"Generous too. How much happiness can a mortal handle? But please go easy on references to crystals or rocks. For some reason, it makes me go all cold and hard inside. Well, there is more to confess...I took advantage of your hypnotized state."

Asadu looked at Trijada with love bubbling in his eyes. Trijada looked levelly at her new husband.

"I forgive you, my moon-faced one. I too have something to confess, my sugar-syrup. I was never really hypnotized, perhaps because I don't believe in hypnotism. I hated Trisiras and Pisacha and wanted to escape their clutches. That's why I pretended to be hypnotized. Then I saw you. I always wanted someone who will do exactly what I say. Someone who is used to obeying. The other day, I followed Pisacha when he went into the temple. I overheard enough of what was going on. When I saw you coming toward Pisacha's room, I hurried back in and pretended as though I knew nothing. Do you think you can find it in your heart to forgive me?"

Some of the bubbles in Asadu's eyes had popped by now. "Not at... at all," stammered Asadu. "There is nothing to forgive."

"I have poured out my half of the milk, but if you drink up your half, it will give you strength. You must make sure to eat those floating bits of saffron."

The vision of his mother forcing him to drink his milk rose unbidden in Asadu's mind. "I hate milk. I probably have some kind of allergy to it..."

Asadu stopped when he saw the steely look in her eyes.

"It's all in your mind. It must be your prejudice and intolerance that is showing up."

"All right. All right. Give it to me. Maybe I will drink just a little bit."

"That's my man," said Trijada, as she put the glass of milk to Asadu's lips. "This will make hair grow on your—"

Asadu winced. 'My man' or more exactly 'my little man' was the phrase his mother used, especially while making him do something that he didn't want to do.

"Wait," cried Asadu.

"—I was about to say, chest. What's wrong, sweetie?"

"Why did you give me the milk with your left hand? Why can't you use the right hand for the right purpose, as God intended?"

"Darling, it's because I am left-handed."

"Left...left-handed?"

Asadu's world seemed to be crumbling. He sat down on the bed with hands on his head. He cheered up a bit gradually. *I still have much to feel lucky about. I have a wife who is fair as the moon.*

"Darling, there is something else I want to tell you. I know you think my face is far too pale and white. Don't worry. It's only because Pisacha and Trisiras had a thing for fair maidens that I wore all this makeup. I will wash it off and underneath you will find a glorious wheatish complexion, almost as good as Ponni's. Or is 'my little man' one of those people who think dark is ugly?" She had her hands on her hips now.

"No, No... Not at all." Asadu managed to mutter.

CHAPTER FIFTY-THREE

THANKSGIVING

"Come in."

The shout came from inside Daivagan's house, even before Ponni raised the brass knocker at the door. Bana, Kalla and Madavi trooped in first. Ponni hung back a little to accompany Vikram, who was tying Chetak and Uchchi to the bars of a front window. Vikram and Ponni hurried to catch up with the rest.

Daivagan's chamber reverberated with the sound of lineage songs.

For the first time, Vikram saw Daivagan smile broadly and was horrified at the tobacco-stained teeth.

"Apeechiko, we came to thank you for everything."

"You muffed your lines," whispered Bana.

"Thanks to you, my brother and Bana were saved from blindness. All of Orum is indebted to you. Thank you for showing us the way."

"You are not done as yet, you know." He turned to Bana. "Bana, people are going to flock to see the play you will write based on your experiences." He then looked again at Vikram.

"You and your friends are not done with your adventures. You shall have many more."

"You heard that," Chetak told Uchchi. "Sorry, I forgot that you don't speak human. We are going to have more adventures."

Uchchi batted her eyelashes. "You seem like a cool equine to hang out with. Tell me again about how you tricked the Brahmarakshas."

CHAPTER FIFTY-FOUR

THE END

Dwipada stayed with Durga and Kuyavan. Durga brought him steaming broth every morning. Jabala stayed at his bedside, practically all day long.

One morning, Dwipada felt there was extra joy in the air. The aroma from the kitchen told him that food was only minutes away. All seemed right with the world. He sprang up from his bed. The sight of Madavi and Kalla greeted him.

"I see that you are feeling well, apeechiko," said Kalla.

"I am feeling great. And you two obviously want something from me."

"Yes," said Madavi. "Kalla has this great opportunity to really impress the guild and get ahead in life. We were hoping that you will be able to help him."

"Anything for you, Madavi. Ask and you shall receive. Though I am not sure that I have anything left to give you."

"It is in your power, master. We just need you to tell the guild elders that Kalla played a major role in the... er... abstraction of the Chintamani."

"You want me, a sage devoted to truth, to tell a lie?" Dwipada's voice was flat.

"Yes, apeechiko," said Madavi.

"All right, consider it done. In any case, the moment I held Chintamani at the temple, I knew it had to be used for a larger purpose. If it serves another purpose, why not? I wouldn't anyway be telling an outright lie, would I?"

"Yes apeechiko, thank you very much. I am eternally in your debt." Kalla's voice caught in his throat as he said this.

The news of what Dwipada had done at Orum reached the ashram before he did.

Aiyo received him with a garland of vagai flowers in her hands and tears in her eyes.

"I am proud of you," she said.

"I am happy I have fulfilled the purpose of my birth. However, I am yet to fulfill my promise to take you on a honeymoon, one you would never have dreamed of."

"Don't worry, lord of my life. I believe your powers have been used for a far nobler cause. I am content."

Dwipada's eyes twinkled with mischief.

"Perhaps, I have some reserves in my tank," he said and snapped his fingers.

Where Dwipada and Aiyo had stood, two elephants appeared. One was a tall tusker and the other a handsome female elephant. The male winked at the female. The female ran toward the forest with a skip and a jump in her gait. The tusker followed at a run. Soon, they disappeared into the forest.

Made in the USA
Charleston, SC
23 September 2016